YUCATÁN

TRANSLATED FROM THE ITALIAN BY

WILLIAM WEAVER

YUCATÁN

ANDREA DE CARLO

HARCOURT BRACE JOVANOVICH, PUBLISHERS

San Diego   New York   London

HBJ

Library of Congress Cataloging-in-Publication Data
De Carlo, Andrea, 1952–
Yucatán/by Andrea De Carlo; translated from the Italian by
William Weaver.—1st ed.
p.   cm.
ISBN 0-15-199895-7
I. Title.
PQ4864.E236Y8313   1990
853'.914—dc20   89-19768

Designed by Joy Chu
Printed in the United States of America
First United States edition
A B C D E

To G. and G.

You've missed the point completely, Julia:
There *were* no tigers. *That* was the point.

T. S. Eliot, *The Cocktail Party*

YUCATÁN

It's fairly typical to be waiting

It's fairly typical to be waiting for Dru Resnik, here, now, at Heathrow. Almost all his films begin or end in an airport; I read somewhere that it's a symbol of the temporary, casual character of life, or something of the sort. Maybe it's also one of the devices that every director at his level uses to make his things immediately identifiable and to provide work for critics and semiprofessional interpreters.

In any event, I pace back and forth so that I can keep as much of the entrance as possible within eyeshot, and in five minutes he arrives, with his wife, Verena, and one of his big suitcases on wheels. Even at a distance, he has this look of the great international artist: there's something in his walk, in the cut of his clothes, the fabrics. When you see his disheveled

1

hair, his nervous feet in tennis shoes, he seems younger than his age, forty-two; but at the same time, it's clear he's not. He's too visibly the possessor of an acknowledged talent, too much more preoccupied than the other travelers, and more alert to himself, as he comes across the great hall.

He shakes my hand and says, "Dave! I'm glad you're coming along, by God!"

"I'm glad, too," I say.

He points to the bag over my shoulder, says, "You've got to explain to me how you manage to travel so light."

I look at his suitcase rolling along on its wheels: I believe his wife packs for him, imagining many more social and climatic events than could happen, even to him.

His wife smiles at me as if I were a superior servant, and immediately looks past me, her eyes apprehensive. She is a tall, handsome woman, slightly rigid in her manner, a former model, German. Dru lets her go ahead as if he doesn't intend to follow her, then he follows her, tense, probably after some scene in the taxi on their way here. And he doesn't like flying at all, he's afraid of planes.

Verena leans toward the girl at the check-in counter, asks for information, confirming what she has already been told. The girl answers in a tone of backward politeness, sees Dru and immediately activates her gaze, goes to the extent of smiling.

Dru says, "I have to make a call"; he slips away. Verena forces me to come with her to the VIP lounge and join her in a coffee. She starts talking to me with great concern about fireplaces she can't remove or replace in the living room without destroying a wall. I want to tell her I work with her husband in order to learn filmmaking, I'm not interested in her problems of interior decoration. Moreover, at every sen-

2

tence she breaks off, looks around, checks the glass door. She always resumes talking at the exact point where she stopped, but I can't keep up with her; I look at her elegant hands, her tapering fingers.

Dru enters, asks for a cup of coffee, comes over to sit down. He takes a sip, says, "Dishwater." It's all too clear the phone call is still on his mind; he doesn't even make an effort to dissimulate. Verena combs her hair back with her fingers, eyes her husband's expression; luckily, she doesn't continue the fireplace story.

The loudspeakers repeat two or three times the invitation for us to board, but Dru doesn't move, he remains frozen in the absence of conversation. He springs up at the last possible moment; we run outside. Verena follows us as far as the electronic gate; she stands there, waving intermittent good-byes until we are definitively around a corner.

There are solar rays through the windows to my right, gusts of pressurized air, a clinking of glasses behind the curtains. It's not bad here in first, with all this space in front and behind and on either side, the stewardesses coming back every two minutes to smile and pour us champagne if we want it. The other passengers are old and rich, covered with foulard scarves and watches and designer shoes, inert and absent in their big seats. The only relatively young person besides me and Dru is a trampy brunette seated next to a real toad of a man: every time I turn, she's there looking back at me, as if I were admiring her.

Dru sinks into his usual flying manner; a slight variation in the sound of the engines or a minimal shift in direction makes him stiffen. But you have to know him to be aware of this; to a stranger he probably seems downright bored, the way he leans on one elbow, his eyes half-closed. He turns, says to me, "Maybe you want to know something about this trip."

"Well, yes," I say. Here my job requires some pretense: an attitude of flexible attention, part technician and part friend, to switch on or off, according to the flow of information. I don't believe there are many other ways of communicating with Dru, especially when you're his assistant.

He says, "It's a picture I've been thinking about for years. Since before I left Yugoslavia."

I say "Ah," prepare to wait. I don't get all that much pleasure out of this sort of conversation. It's like walking with somebody who drags his feet and stops or breaks into a run or turns back or decides to go on for miles without even thinking of telling you what he has in mind. Before he left Yugoslavia means at least seven years ago. I was sixteen or seventeen; I saw his films in little art houses filled with cinemaniacs. The films were low-budget and short, but light-years away from everything you would see normally. I don't believe Dru gave much thought to the public or to the critics then, even though he had already become a cult figure outside his native country. I don't believe he imagined he would end up at the center of a highly organized financial machine like the one surrounding him now, or that he would be so universally approved and revered no matter what he did. But maybe, on the contrary, he spent his time imagining just that; it's hard to say.

He says, "I don't know if you've heard of Astor Camado, the writer."

"Yes," I say, trying to think fast, recalling a couple of dust jackets.

"But have you read him?" Dru says, already assuming his peremptory tone.

"I know the name," I say. This role of the ignorant kid irritates me now, but it's true that I'm not a great consumer of novels. To me they always seem to make a fuss over nothing, to be imprecise, full of pointless descriptions of feelings.

"Anyway," Dru says, "he's written four books, which tell the same story from four different points of view. The story: a young New York musicologist of South American extraction goes to Mexico to do some research and meets this Indian witch doctor, who little by little draws him into a vortex of magic practices, until he's brought into contact with a world beyond, or a parallel world, if you like."

I nod, yes. I understand the *kind* of film, apart from the story.

Dru says, "I've always thought it could make an incredible picture. There's his gradual moving away from the scientific rationality where he used to take refuge, and these landscapes all made of lights and minerals in the pure state, these strange characters, hard to figure out, like pre-Columbian figures. It's a story of emotional states, of perspectives more than of acts. There are some extraordinary descriptions of *voids*, of obscure fears and desires." He looks out the window, worried as the wing dips a little.

I continue displaying attention, and I wait. After the incredible success of his last two films, it mustn't be all that easy to think up something. The pressure must be great, on all sides.

"Camado is a strange story in himself," he says. "His books have sold millions of copies, but nobody's ever managed to photograph him or interview him or discover who he really is. Every time I've tried to contact him to ask for the film rights, somebody's told me a different version. First, that he had gone crazy on all that peyote and mescaline and was

5

living like a zombie in some Colombian forest; then, that he was dead; then, that he was alive but wanted ten million dollars for each of his four books; and then, that he didn't even exist and was only a name invented for a big publishing operation. This last version was told to me by the wife of the president of Mexico, at a dinner party in Paris. Even Camado's agent swore he knew nothing about the man and received the manuscripts in the mail."

A cute black stewardess comes and fills my glass; she tries to attract Dru's attention, holds up the champagne bottle; she retreats when he signals no, hardly looking at her.

Dru says, "Then last month Jack Nesbitt called me. For a couple of years now he's had the idea of producing a film of mine. He has an incredible amount of money he inherited from his father, an oilman, and though he doesn't seem to know much about movies, he has this persistent enthusiasm for me. I've talked to him about Camado on occasion, and apparently Jack's managed to find him and persuade him to give me the rights. So now there should be this historic meeting with the great Astor, to talk a bit and also to hop down to Mexico with him and look at the scenes of the books."

I'm still acting alert, but Dru doesn't say anything else, and goes back to looking out the window. I get up to stretch my legs, I go and chat with the cute black stewardess. She laughs, asks me where I bought my shoes, if we're going to the States to make a movie or what. She points to Dru, sitting up ahead, says we should look her up the first time we're in Boston and she's not flying. I say I don't know about Dru, but I surely will; even though he's the one, of course, who interests her.

Finally we're flying low over Los Angeles, at night; we're on the runway; out of the plane and down the escalators along with dozens of rumpled passengers anxious to get away and sleep.

In the area where the baggage carousels are revolving, a man of about thirty-five starts waving to us from a distance of fifty feet; big smiles as he comes toward us. He grips Dru's hand, says to him, "How was the flight?"

"Mm," Dru says. He introduces me, says, "Dave Hollis, my assistant. Jack Nesbitt."

Nesbitt shakes my hand, says, "Hi there, Dave." He's full of dynamic energy, he has a big head on a thick neck, a blue cashmere jacket, a wristwatch with many hands. He takes the suitcase away from Dru the moment Dru lifts it from the carousel, drags it toward the exit. Outside, he opens the doors of a big black Mercedes, helps me put the bags in the trunk. He takes his place behind the wheel, makes sure Dru and I are all set, then drives off along a semicircular exit road.

Dru points to the car, says, "Like a genuine Hollywood tycoon."

Nesbitt looks at him, says, "No, it's just comfortable, mostly. . . ."

"Of course," Dru says. He's good at undermining the confidence of confident people; it's a kind of instinct he has.

Nesbitt glides onto the freeway, in the steady flow of cars. He checks Dru, glancing at him; says, "I had lunch with Astor. He can't wait to meet you."

"What's he like?" Dru says.

"*Very* agreeable," Nesbitt says. "Witty, too. Not at all the guru type, the hermit you might expect. And he's *crazy* about the idea of the picture. He says he's always been an admirer of yours; if he had known you were interested in his books, he'd have come to you."

Dru doesn't seem very impressed; he taps a finger on the

7

arm of the seat. He says, "Can we be sure it's really him? Not just somebody playing the part?"

Nesbitt tries to study him in the intermittent light, laughs, says, "Dru, you think I'd have you come all the way here to meet some crook? I've made ten trips to New York, to talk with his agent, Gene Baker. This is the genuine article. Guaranteed."

"Magnificent," Dru says.

Nesbitt keeps on giving him quick, sidelong glances; he changes lanes. He says, "I'm sure you'll like him, Dru."

Dru looks at the lights of Westwood without great interest; he hums a little tune they were playing in the arrivals lounge.

The ridiculous thing

The ridiculous thing is that every time, after ambushes and long waits and false starts and repeated overtures, I finally manage to make contact with a story that has fascinated me, I am filled with this immediate disappointment. I still don't have a clear idea of what it really is, seen up close, but already it seems to me ten times simpler and flatter than what I thought I saw, and with none of the nuances and twists and secret depths I had imagined from a distance. I go on for months and years, trying to convince everyone that it's something extraordinary, I underline and simplify and amplify sensations until someone believes in it and goes and gets it for me and puts it in front of me, then steps aside waiting for me to make use of it for something at least proportionate to the energy he invested to procure it for me; and instead of being pleased I stand there looking at it full of embarrassment and alienation. I feel like someone who rents a house by mail on the basis of the vaguest description, and, without ever having set foot in it, plans encounters and dinners and parties of every sort in its rooms, and the more details he adds to his mental images, the more he reduces the likelihood of their ever corresponding to that setting. And of course it's too late to cancel the lease and go away. The same thing would happen with any other story, and if I were to transfer reflections of this sort to my protagonist, the film would turn out full of self-pity and narcissism, all cramped actions and circular dialogue. I don't think someone like Dave would ever go and see it.

I wake up much too early

I wake up much too early; I need a few days, every time, to get over jet lag. I turn on the TV, look at the fake, pink face of an announcer without hearing what he says. This is a real Hilton room, big and dull and perfectly standardized. I pull open the heavy draperies and then the curtains: there is a pool in the center of the patio, enclosed by two other wings of the hotel and a wall; the sun is still weak, a yellowish white. I shave, stand under the shower for a good fifteen minutes; the sounds of TV commercials penetrate the frosted glass. I get dressed, light things I wore in London two or three months ago. It's rather exciting to be in Los Angeles now, and settled so comfortably.

The corridor is padded, every footstep muffled. I stop at

Dru's door, but can't hear anything. He's probably shaving, or telephoning in a whisper to some of his women in London, to reassure them or keep them uncertain or tense. Or else he's asleep. He always insists that he wakes up very early, but this may be just another of his many ways of making others feel guilty.

The lobby is humming, compared with last night: managerial staff dressed in gray or blue, old cream-colored couples, and Middle Eastern businessmen on the phone, leaning against a wall, or else engaged in arguments while they study the watches and belts in the hotel shops.

I go down to a still-lower level, where there are a couple of bars and restaurants, a hairdresser, a travel agency. It's not so much a hotel as a kind of enclosed city; you could live here, never sticking your nose outside.

I have breakfast in one of the cafés. I order almost everything there is on the menu, more for the fun of ordering than because I'm hungry. The waitresses are Hispanics; they flash by with their trays. The air and the light are artificial, carefully controlled; there is some music kept very low.

When I finish, I call Dru on one of the phones in the corridor. He answers at the first ring, says, "Ah, yes, Dave, we'll meet in the lobby at noon." He spends hours on the phone, but doesn't like being called; he takes it as an intrusion every time. I only hope I won't go through life as an assistant director.

I go out into the patio with the pool, on the fake plastic grass that covers the concrete. There are three or four people sunbathing on the deck chairs at the edge of the water. An ugly girl with tiny eyes is seated behind a big glass counter displaying suntan lotions and swimming articles. I point to some trunks, a pair of goggles. She produces them, asks if it'll be cash or charged to the room. I tell her to charge them; I don't believe it'll make much difference to Nesbitt. I swim for a good half hour, at a steady pace in the warm water. From Wilshire Boulevard, just beyond the wall comes the sweetish smell of exhaust fumes, made even sweeter by the light and the temperature.

I go up to our floor again, and Dru is at his door, looking out with a puzzled expression. He says, "I was waiting for you. Take a look at this." He hands me a piece of paper, observes my reactions.

There are two lines, in pencil, written in a shaky and sprawling hand; they say: *Attention, wrongly directed, is dangerous, because it rebounds. We are watching you.*

Dru says, "Who can this be, do you think? I found it on the floor."

"I have no idea," I say. The paper is hotel letterhead; there's a supply in every room and also down in the lobby.

Dru stares at me with a suspicious glint in his eyes, says, "You didn't write it, by any chance?"

I laugh, to establish my distance from the idea, say, "What put that into your head?"

"Oh, nothing," he says, looking down the corridor.

I hand the paper back to him. Actually, he could easily have written it himself. He always has this tendency to alter details of the furnishings and the lights, as if he were on a set; to heighten situations in order to make them more interesting, to force people to act with fewer inhibitions than usual.

He folds the paper, puts it in his pocket. He says, "Get a move on. Camado will be here soon."

I go and take off my bathing things, leave them in the room, join him down in the lobby. He's sitting with Nesbitt in a corner with easy chairs; they are talking about contracts,

I guess, but they break off. Nesbitt says to me, "Well, how's it going?" and immediately concentrates on Dru again.

There is a short man dressed in white who walks briskly toward us, with a little cane in his hand.

Nesbitt gets up and greets him with the greatest cordiality, directs him to Dru, makes gestures of introduction: "Dru Resnik, Astor Camado"; he looks from one to the other, half a pace apart, tries to move them closer together.

Camado smiles, shakes Dru's hand, says to him, "A great, great pleasure." When he's finished, he also greets me, says, "You've had a good trip, I hope?" A South American accent, a slightly shrill, rough voice, quick black eyes. After what Dru told me on the plane I imagined him different, thinner, more aloof. On the contrary, he is plump, full of exuberance, as he circles Dru and Nesbitt with his walking stick. He could be forty or even over sixty, dark-skinned and smooth as he is, with sparse eyebrows and coal-black hair.

There are a couple of women, thirtyish, behind him; he turns and introduces them, says, "Kate, Maribel." They are pale and gawky, like a pair of little lay nuns, and they stick close to each other. Maribel says to Dru in a quavering voice, "We've seen all your films twice."

But Dru is paying attention only to Camado. He looks at him close up, touches his arm, says, "You were beginning to turn into a kind of mirage." In situations like this, his Slavic nature seeps through his Anglicization in the form of a more persistent and physical cordiality, more overt.

Nesbitt follows the exchanges between Dru and Camado like a parent who has arranged a meeting between his son and the neighbors' boy. He avoids intervening, lets them talk and study each other; then when their preliminary dialogue seems close to running dry, he says, "What about going to eat? I've made a reservation at Kurini's."

We all go outside under the marquee. For Dru's benefit, Camado makes some remarks about the London climate compared with here. The attendants bring up Nesbitt's car and Camado's: a little white Toyota. It's strange that, after the millions of copies he's sold, he can't afford something better; but perhaps he's frugal by nature, or perhaps, since he has to guard his secrecy so much, he isn't able to handle his contracts carefully, or else he doesn't want to be conspicuous. His clothes, too, are commonplace, like something from a department store.

Dru gets into Camado's Toyota, sends me and the two disciples with Nesbitt, saying, "We'll follow you."

Nesbitt drives slowly, checking in the rearview mirror every few seconds for fear of losing the others. At a red light he asks Maribel, "Where does Astor usually live?"

"I don't know," she says.

Nesbitt says, "But when he's in L.A., does he stay with you two?"

"Only during the day," Kate says. "At our house we can't have men sleep over." She also has a nun's voice, bloodless.

Nesbitt checks to make sure the Toyota is still behind us; he says, "Who gives you these orders? Who decides?"

"Nobody," Kate says.

"They aren't orders," Maribel says.

We pull in among other Mercedeses and Porsches and Ferraris under a pergola of Virginia creeper. The parking attendant looks slightly embarrassed when he sees Camado's car; he takes it off to park it out of sight.

Inside, the decor is all pale hues, with low tables, at which some marketing directors or lawyers or record-company executives are seated, with a TV actress or two, or a woman in advertising. They eat salads, for the most part.

At our table, Dru takes over the seating as always; he makes us sit down and stand up several times until he decides that the juxtapositions are right. He puts Nesbitt at a slight distance, on either side of himself he seats Camado and Maribel, who is the less ugly of the two women, the other he shifts next to me.

A waiter comes and in a coy voice recites the list of dishes, describes the ingredients in the different sauces. Camado says at once, "Lobster for me," without much concern for precedence. He looks at Nesbitt, snickers, asks him some details of another restaurant to which they have been together, says to Dru, "You must get him to take you."

Dru says yes, smiles. It's unusual to see him this interested in someone; as a rule the situation is tilted completely in his favor from the start, even before he opens his mouth. But now he keeps looking at Camado, asks him to explain the title of one of his books, listens without turning away or interrupting him in mid-sentence, as he would do normally. Camado launches into talk that seems almost in code, waving his short arms. In return, immediately afterward, he asks Dru which characters in his latest film are based on real people. Dru says, "They are all cocktails of real people, three or four mixed together, with some unconfessable dreams thrown in, and some unsuccessful thefts."

Kate, at my left, is a true disciple: she concentrates all the time on the other side of the table, barely looks at me. Only, at a certain point, she smiles a little, flaccid smile and says to me, "It must be interesting to be Mr. Resnik's secretary."

I don't even bother to explain, I say, "Very."

The waiter brings our dishes; Camado and the two disciples seem impressed; Dru turns to look at three blonde women at a nearby table. Nesbitt immediately intervenes to keep the conversation alive; he says to Camado, "I remember that when *Encounter with the Void* came out and went straight to the top of the best-seller lists, practically every important paper and magazine in the country sent a reporter to track you down." He turns to Dru, says, "You've no idea. He drove them *crazy*; they couldn't bear not knowing what he looked like."

"I can imagine," Dru says.

Camado extracts the white flesh from the lobster, thrusts it into his mouth with rapid forkfuls. He says, "Once, at that time, some friends and I went to a party in San Francisco, and the host, who didn't have the slightest idea who I was, introduced me to a man who was passing himself off as me." He reaches for the mayonnaise, some lemon, he messes with his dish.

"What did you do then?" Nesbitt says, checking to see if Dru is still interested.

"I shook hands with him," Camado says. "He was a tall, blond guy, fairly handsome but with a stupid look. You should have seen all the women he had around him."

Nesbitt says, "In the end, did you expose him?"

"Are you kidding?" Camado says with his mouth full. "How often do you find somebody willing to attract all the negativity that would otherwise be directed at you?"

Dru laughs, says, "That's true." Nesbitt laughs; Kate and Maribel also, like a pair of sheep.

Before the laughter can leave a gap, Nesbitt says, "What about the lady you told me about yesterday?"

"Ah, yes," Camado says. He has a professional way of remaining the center of attention; I believe he has to make an effort not to monopolize. He says, "Once, in New York, Gene Baker telephones me. He's my agent and more or less the only official person who knows me. He says to me, please come here because I have a problem. So I go to see him, and there's a beautiful lady, about thirty, very elegant and nervous. Gene introduces me, and says to her, I don't know who got you pregnant, madam, but this is the only writer named Astor Camado that I've ever met." He laughs, almost frantically, for a moment, throwing back his little round head.

Dru says, "One thing I've always envied writers: They can work without showing themselves. They can *not* exist."

"Not only writers," Camado says. "*Anyone* can not exist." To say this, he changes his appearance slightly, becomes more serious, grim, straightens up in his chair. He looks hard at Dru, but doesn't add anything.

There is a space of pure fork-wielding; Nesbitt seems hesitant. Maribel says, "The music for *Lines* is magnificent. I've got the cassette and I listen to it every evening."

Dru says, "Really?," not paying much attention.

Kate says, "You know? Five years ago Maribel was about to go blind, but Acambòn took her into the jungle and healed her with macaulino nuts."

From the way she says it, Acambòn sounds like a character in some book of Camado's; maybe I should read them. I'm beginning to feel excluded from the conversation.

Maribel smiles, her eyes rather glassy. Nesbitt says, "Incredible." The waiter brings fruit sorbets.

Then Dru is suddenly fed up with the situation; he says, "We've been sitting here one hour."

"Yes, of course," Nesbitt says, and immediately signals for the check.

Dru looks at Camado, says, "When are you taking us to Mexico?" He now uses his impatient tone, with only some traces of his earlier, cordial curiosity.

"Whenever you like," Camado says. "I'm at your disposal."

"How about tomorrow, then?" Dru says.

"Whenever you like," Camado says again. He accepts the idea of slipping into the background, at least as far as Dru is concerned; he holds his arms out.

Dru says, "Fine." He stands up, shakes his legs as if he had been sitting down a whole day.

Nesbitt hands one of many credit cards to the waiter, says, "Then I'll reserve our seats on the plane."

"It's better if we go by car," Camado says. "We'll be staying in the northern part of the country anyway."

Nesbitt calculates, I believe, the time and cost and energy involved, he says, "It's a long haul, by car."

"But it's better," Camado says. Perhaps he too is afraid of planes, or he's making it a matter of principle, so as not to feel totally subordinated.

"We'll do what Astor prefers," Dru says; he heads for the door.

Nesbitt says, "Okay," takes back his credit card.

Outside, we walk a few paces, vaguely, among the parked cars. Dru draws Camado aside, shows him the message found in his room. Camado takes just a glance, smiles, shakes his head. He says, "I don't pay attention anymore. I get them by the dozen." He speaks of this as if it were something that concerned only him; he says, "There are a lot of lunatics around; they consider themselves followers of Camado only because they've read a couple of my books, they follow me everywhere, they try to intrude."

The attendant brings the white Toyota back from wherever he had hidden it; Maribel and Kate slip inside, wave their hands briefly to say good-bye. Camado says he'll meet us in the hotel at eight to discuss the trip some more. He shakes everybody's hand with an only slightly attenuated replica of the cordiality of our meeting; he drives off.

Nesbitt takes us back toward Beverly Hills; we are all lulled by the barely perceptible hum of the engine. He says, "Well? Is he likable, or not?"

"Very," Dru says.

Verena would probably

Verena would probably say that at the bottom of everything there's an attempt to escape responsibility, and she would fill me with rage as usual, and as usual she would be partly right, but only partly. The fact is that no matter how hard I try to establish some equilibrium between the people who interest me and the various components of my work and places and times and objects, in the end it's always a fake equilibrium, irregular, composed of internal differences and arranged to compensate for them with the help of little levers and hidden counter-weights. It's an equilibrium of guilt feelings and future plans and promises and insincere assurances, far more than of actual facts. Nobody would dare consider it a foundation for other structures. It's a complex, precarious achievement that cannot be utilized; the moment I go away, it cracks and begins to crumble; when I come back, I have to start over from scratch, abandoning the other fake equilibrium I was constructing in the meanwhile with whatever material was at hand. And there doesn't seem to be much of that just now, with Dave so caught up in his own role and Jack so full of mechanical enthusiasm, and the only people I can talk with all on the other side of the ocean and attached to an equilibrium that is surely already deteriorating fast.

Sometimes I wonder how my films must seem to a person like Dave, with his implacable sensitivity to the flow of the surface, the definition of details, and his total lack of sympathy with any instability or hesitation that might lie beneath. And the sixteen- and eighteen-year-olds who go to the movies today must be even farther ahead; they must see a story as you see a clock or pistol or any other mechanism assembled to perform a function as efficiently as possible. Nesbitt doesn't give it much thought, he's so convinced that he only has to pull out some money and hook up with my name to have himself carried along through Oscar night and then to international glory. And Camado, who seems so pleased that I want to take his story and dismantle it and then put it back together with different materials arranged in a different way, pieces removed and pieces added, but still miraculously ticking and actually more effective and poetic and profitable even than the original. I don't believe I would ever have set out in such insistent pursuit of this film if I had known that, in the end, I would catch up with it.

I must have fallen asleep

I must have fallen asleep, because outside it's dark and it's already seven; the TV has continued on its own; somebody knocks at the door. Sleeping in the daytime stupefies me completely; I try not to do it, ever. I go to the door.

Dru comes in, turns off the TV, hands me a sheet of paper.

The handwriting is the same as that of the other message: an uneven pencil scrawl on the page. It says: *Those who, instead of trying to understand, only seek confirmation of what they think they know, run the greatest risk. We are watching you.*

Dru takes back the paper, says, "Whoever it is, he's beginning to annoy me."

I slip on my shoes, try to clear my head. I say, "Where was it?"

"On the floor of my room, like the other," Dru says; he puts the paper back in the envelope, which has his name on it, spelled with a *c* before the *k*.

I follow him out into the corridor; we look at the closed door of his room. He says, "It was at least six feet from the door. I can't figure out how the hell they managed to push it so far inside."

I say to him, "Let's try." I make him give me the envelope, I try to slip it under the door: it won't go. I flatten it, but it still won't. There is no space between the wood of the door and the carpet.

Dru looks at me, and his bewilderment is turning into real concern. He says, "What does it mean, then? They came into the room?"

"I don't know," I say. "In any case, they didn't slip it inside." It's odd, now, this story. I can't figure it out.

A waiter with a dark face goes by, pushing a trolley of clean towels. Dru turns to watch him until he disappears around a corner of the corridor; then he says, "Maybe it's one of them; they all must have passkeys."

I say, "Maybe so," give him back the envelope. He weighs it in his hand; he reopens his door, says, "All right, we'll meet downstairs in half an hour."

I go wash my face, watch part of an idiotic quiz show on TV. It wouldn't be half bad to be here by myself, for a film of my own; I'd only like to know how many decades have to go by before that'll be possible. I put on a jacket, go downstairs.

Dru and Nesbitt are sitting in one of the bars, puzzled. Dru says, "According to Jack, it could be somebody connected in some way with the same witch doctor as Camado's."

"It's just an idea," Nesbitt says, with a gesture to make it less important.

Dru says, "Of course, it's possible. Maybe somebody's annoyed that Camado told about things that were supposed to remain secret, and now he actually wants to let us make a movie about them."

"Or somebody's jealous because he was excluded," Nesbitt says, to put Camado in a better light.

We stay in the bar drinking white wine, waiting for eight o'clock. Nesbitt describes, somewhat uneasily, a couple of projects he's considering: a technological Western and a comedy with an actor Dru loathes. It's obvious Nesbitt doesn't know much about movies, but he's good at financial calculations, evaluating the market.

At eight we go up to the lobby. Camado is already there waiting for us, pacing up and down near the front desk. He greets us one by one, leans on his cane. Nesbitt points to it: "Beautiful."

"It's a stick of power," Camado says; he raises it just slightly.

Dru says to him, "I found another message in my room."

Camado doesn't seem surprised; he says, "If I showed you all the notes and letters I get, you'd laugh."

"But who can it be?" Nesbitt says.

Camado says, "It's all these lunatics. The world's full of lunatics." From the way he looks at Dru it's possible that Camado would nevertheless like to know what the new message says, but he doesn't ask.

Nesbitt says, "Why don't we go and eat?"

We go up to the top floor, where there is a deluxe restaurant, with gilt and red plush, just as you step out of the elevator. The maître d' looks at us; you can't go in without a jacket. The only one without a jacket is Camado; he's wearing the boyish white windbreaker he had on this morning. Nesbitt asks the maître d' if he can't lend Camado a

25

jacket; the maître d' says no. Beyond him we can glimpse one corner of the room, with middle-aged ladies in long evening dresses, alert waiters gliding by. Nesbitt insists; I don't think he's ever in his whole life been turned away from a restaurant; the maître d' continues blocking our path, in the attitude of a man guarding morality. Dru watches, then is bored; he says to the maître d': "Who gives a shit about eating in this cheap whorehouse? You can go to hell, you and all your whores." He raises his voice a bit; the maître d' blanches, a passing waiter looks around.

In the elevator, Nesbitt is embarrassed; he says, "I'm sorry. It's ridiculous."

"Pigs," Dru says. Camado remains silent, looks at his fingernails.

Nesbitt says there should be a Hawaiian restaurant below. We cross the lobby, walk past a big store, go down a stairway. There is a long underground corridor with arrows and signs, ALOHA ROOM, a kind of tunnel for residents, who can avoid exposure to the open air even for a few steps.

A Japanese-looking maître d' bows to us at the doorway; he says we can't come in without jackets. Now we all turn toward Camado; Dru says, "Why, this is *persecution*." Camado doesn't seem amused; he can only produce a very stiff little smile. But this maître d' has jackets available; he has one brought at once. Camado hands over his white windbreaker as if it were a hostage, slips on the jacket reluctantly: a blue admiral's coat, too wide and too long for him, with a gilt-thread coat of arms on the breast pocket.

The maître d' guides us to the most distant, shadowy table, signals to summon a waiter. The place is almost empty; there are only a pair of silent couples in the dim light. A dugout canoe hangs from the fake beams of the ceiling; plastic lobsters and fish are trapped in fake nets on the walls. There is soft Hawaiian music: guitars that emit long twangs. We order dishes at random, without much interest. The atmosphere isn't easy; several years seem to have gone by since noon today. Camado says he wants only water, he never eats in the evening. He is sitting a bit lower than us, engulfed in the admiral's blue jacket; he looks at the table.

Nesbitt asks him about tomorrow's trip into Mexico. Camado says he's thought it over and we have to go in two cars, he and Dru in one, Nesbitt and I in the other. He doesn't seem to want to explain why; he takes his iced Perrier in both hands, has them bring a straw. He says, "If we all four go in one car, the two in the back will fall asleep."

"Why should they do that?" Nesbitt says. He makes an effort to be understanding, looks at Dru.

"Because they won't see much," Camado says. "The road is all curves." He looks stubborn and irrational now, hard to budge.

Nesbitt says, "I can't understand. . . . "

"I'm the only one who knows this road," Camado says. He stares into his glass, trying to close the discussion.

Dru seems intrigued by this deaf stubbornness, by Nesbitt's polite dismay; he keeps out of the debate.

Nesbitt says, "Astor, I swear to you: I've never gone to sleep in a car in my life. I'll sit in the back. Me and Dave. It doesn't make sense for us to split up."

"Yes, it does," Camado says without looking at him.

Finally, Dru speaks up, says, "It seems simpler to me if we all go together, Astor." In things like this he is very much a director, he knows when artistic irrationality must give way to organizational reality. Nesbitt looks at him with relief, takes a sip of wine. Camado says, "Whatever you say," stirs the ice with his straw.

We're silent for a few minutes, we eat the fake Hawaiian

27

food, semisweet and bland. Then Dru starts questioning Camado about his books, much more serious and systematic than he was today at noon. He asks him about details, has the mechanism of certain rituals explained, wants to know the meaning of individual words. Each time, Camado allows the question to settle, then he answers in a low voice, his elbows on the table. The exchange is slow, heavy, not at all friendly.

After a while, Dru says, "But what if I had to *describe* the world beyond?"

"A completely empty, dark room," Camado says. The tone of his voice, too, is different from today at noon, deeper. He says, "There's nothing to recognize, nothing happens. There is only this absolute blackness."

Dru pushes his plate away, says, "To be sure, it's terrible."

"Why terrible?" Camado says. He no longer has the slightest trace of cordiality, he seems remote, worried; I don't know if the lighting and the decor of this place have something to do with it. He says, "'Terrible' presupposes a series of references that no longer have any meaning in that phase. 'Terrible' compared to what? A dark room can frighten you if you compare it constantly to the outside, to the open air and the light, but if the dark room is all there is, you no longer have a point of view from which the dark room is terrible."

Dru nods his head. Nesbitt, I believe, is trying to imagine how this talk can be translated into a movie that can be shown in theaters.

Camado says, "The secret is knowing that absolutely *everything* is insignificant: love and activity and relationships and feelings, landscapes, desires, plans, et cetera. They're nothing but bric-a-brac, little pieces of kitsch scattered around. The secret is *not to be there*. You understand what I mean?"

"Yes," Dru says, even though I don't believe it's all that clear to him, either. But he has this air of concentration, he really is making an effort to follow Camado.

"For example, now I'm here, but I'm not here," Camado says. He uses the right tone, manages not to be ridiculous, manages to make us imagine other meanings behind his words. Probably he has had a lot of experience with this sort of thing, he's worked at it a long time. He says, "I could be any other place, and it would be the same thing. La Huela, for example, once reproached Kate because she worried too much about being loved by other people."

"Who's La Huela?" Nesbitt says. He's beginning to look alarmed by this talk; I bet he hasn't read Camado's books all that much himself.

But Camado is addressing only Dru; he continues, ignoring this interruption; he says, "She told her it's *insignificant,* being loved or not; you shouldn't have such a confining point of view, as if everything had to flow to you because of what you think you are. The things that seem important to you don't *exist.* It's all a spinning in the void."

Dru looks at him, remains silent.

Camado says, "But until we realize it, we continue running around, expending energy on human relations, and we make plans and we dash here and there, seeking confirmation of our feelings, deluding ourselves that they correspond to universal states suspended above us; we can't even accept the *idea* of absolute nothingness."

Now nobody is saying anything, or eating anything. The waiter comes to clear away the plates. Camado sucks his water very slowly; the level in his glass seems always the same. Nesbitt and I look at each other with a kind of ceremonial demeanor, as if we had happened by mistake into a service of some obscure religion. Dru taps his fingers on the table.

Then Nesbitt pays the check; we stand up. We retrace our way through the tunnel, still oppressed and slowed down by the atmosphere of the restaurant, not looking at one another. When we are again in the lobby, things immediately improve, with all the lights and the sounds and the movements of the guests and patrons of the hotel in their many activities. Camado, by contrast, seems to lose weight, to walk less certainly. He says good-bye, that he'll be back tomorrow morning to go to Mexico. We look at him as he goes off with his little stick of power.

Nesbitt walks me and Dru toward the elevators. Dru says to him, "Are you still sure you want to make this picture, Jack?"

"Of course," Nesbitt says. He tries to remove the puzzlement from his face, says, "It all seems absolutely fascinating to me."

The telephone rings imperiously

The telephone rings imperiously; Dru's voice says, "Were you sleeping?"

"No, no," I say. In reality I'm at a crucial moment in a movie on cable; I try to keep watching the screen.

Dru says, "There's another message. If you come here, you can see it."

I take just one more glance, to get an idea of the possible developments. It's not a great picture, but it always irritates me to leave a story halfway through.

Dru lets me in, looks down the corridor both ways before he closes the door and hands me the paper. On the bed his suitcase is lying open, almost ready.

The usual writing on the usual hotel paper says: *Only a fool asks a man who was stopped at the gate to describe the house. We are watching you.*

Dru paces back and forth, says, "Can you figure out what the hell they want from me?"

"No," I say. "They don't seem to be asking anything specific."

Dru draws the curtain, opens it again. It's odd how this room has the exact same furniture and dimensions and fabrics as mine, and yet it isn't the same at all. There seems to be much more of it, even though I can't say why; maybe only because of the nonchalance with which the air has been stirred.

Dru comes away from the window; he says, "Unless it's Nesbitt, who wants to have me make a different picture, or Camado, who's trying to upset us or test us."

I look at the cover of one of Camado's books, in the open suitcase: a red sunset in a desert.

Dru slips on a jacket, says, "All right, let's go downstairs and get something to eat."

We go out into the corridor, and two men heading toward us stop short. They are perhaps thirty feet away: one is very short and stocky, the other blond and tall, both dressed in three-piece gray suits, like businessmen. They remain motionless, a still photograph, for at least a couple of seconds, then slowly look at each other, turn, and retrace their steps, gaining speed as they go off; they vanish around the corner.

Dru seems about to take a breath or to start laughing; instead, he shouts, "Would you mind doing that just one more time?"

I don't know why he shouts that, among all the things he could shout, but in any case the short and stocky one peers around the corner again almost immediately, looks at us with an uncertain smile, as if really on the point of repeating the whole thing. The other guy reaches out with one arm and pulls him away.

Dru and I stand there looking at the empty corridor, an ash receptacle just before the corner. When we run to the end, there is nobody there anymore; the little green arrows of the elevators are pointing down. Dru runs one hand through his hair, says nothing.

It's a few minutes before we get down to the lobby; we take a turn around it, but naturally the two men have vanished. We go into one of the cafés, have some coffee, look around. Dru says, "They didn't seem to be lunatics." He takes the last message out of his pocket, but it isn't any easier to interpret now. He says, "I wonder if they were bringing me another." The receptionist looks at us from her place near the door, and she also seems suspect, her hair the color of dried straw, her eyeglasses with little round lenses.

Just as we get up, Nesbitt arrives. His face is tense; he says, "Astor called me. Yesterday evening, when he left here, a car followed him."

Dru says, "What?" He makes Nesbitt repeat his words several times. We are blocking the way among the tables, forcing the waiters to flatten themselves against the wall to slide past us. Dru shows Nesbitt the latest message, tells him about the two guys in the corridor. Nesbitt says, "Oh, shit."

We go up to the lobby level, suspicious among other people. Nesbitt says, "I think we'd better inform the police."

Camado comes up behind us, from a side entrance. He barely greets us, looks in several directions, full of alarm. He says, "Let's go somewhere less crowded."

We go back down to the lower level. Nesbitt points to four

easy chairs in a blind corner. Camado shakes his head, looking around for someplace else. We go to the end of the corridor; Camado pushes open a glass door, leading to the patio with the pool; he says, "Out here perhaps."

We go out on the plastic grass. The sun is strong, all four of us narrow our eyes. There are about ten people in the deck chairs, the girl behind the glass swimming-articles stand is completely absorbed in reading a book entitled *Interferences*. Camado walks along the edge of the pool, stops in a patch of shadow, where it would be hard for anyone to overhear us. Dru says to him, "Well?"

Camado looks around again, says, "As soon as I came out of the garage, I realized they were following me, because they had two cars and they kept always the same distance, fifty feet, behind; I tried changing speed a couple of times and I broke at least a dozen laws, but there was no shaking them off." He speaks nervously, stops, checks the patio. It's incredible how last night's detachment has dissolved and its place has been taken by all these human reactions, after all his talk about not being there, et cetera.

Dru and Nesbitt are aghast, speechless.

Camado says, "They were professionals, all right. You just had to see the way they stuck to me, until I stopped at a police station and ran inside. At that point they vanished."

Nesbitt says, "But why were they tailing you, do you think?"

Camado shakes his round head; he says, "How should I know?" He's almost pathetic now, little, filled with fear.

"And you haven't the slightest idea who it could be?" Nesbitt says.

"No," Camado says without looking at him. "It could be the CIA, or some criminal, or anybody. *Anybody*."

We are standing in the patch of shade, close together, like four conspirators; one step toward the pool and we are in full sunlight, dazzled.

Dru tells Camado about the latest message and the two guys in the corridor, and Camado reels for a moment. He has these dark, lively eyes; they show a little flash of concentrated panic.

Nesbitt says, "Maybe we could sit down, at least." He points to some white chairs a few feet away; I help him carry them into the shade.

Camado reluctantly sits on the edge of his, says, "Dru, the fact is that the place and the moment are *wrong*. Maybe it would have been different if we were meeting in London, or even here but in some other situation. But right now, it's wrong." He no longer pays any attention to his tone; he seems to want only to get out of the whole business as quickly as possible.

"Wrong? How?" Dru says.

Camado shifts his stick of power from one hand to the other; he says, "It's hard to explain, Dru. It's dangerous."

Dru says, "And going to Mexico is dangerous, too?"

"Yes," Camado says. "The only thing is to give up the idea."

Nesbitt holds out his palms, says, "Wait a minute, Astor; let's try to use our heads. Dru came all the way out here only for this reason. We had agreed; we've been talking about it for months; it's all set. . . . "

"I'm sorry," Camado says. "It's not my fault. It's nobody's fault."

Nesbitt huddles down in his seat; he says, "I can't believe it, Astor; this is absurd. You can't do a thing like this to us, now of all times. You can't destroy this whole project because of a couple of anonymous messages from some crank who's heard Dru's in town and staying in this hotel."

Camado says, again, "I'm sorry; it's the wrong moment." He is all contracted, clutching his cane; it's obvious there's no hope of making him change his mind.

Nesbitt looks at Dru, seeking help; but Dru is fascinated by the change in Camado. Nesbitt gets up, takes two or three steps, without moving away; he says, "And now what do we do? Go to Mexico on our own?"

"If you go by yourselves, there's no risk," Camado says at once. He glimpses a way out, says, "I can explain to you where, and you can easily go on your own."

"And there's no risk?" Dru says.

"Absolutely not," Camado says. Now that he feels almost safe, he also tries to go back a step and resume his role, recover at least a part of his tone of last night. He says, "The fact is that if I come along, then *you* are in danger. I have an umbrella that protects me; I don't have to worry about anything. But it's not big enough for all four of us; that's the truth of the matter. What happens if, for example, Dave here remains outside?" He points to me, as if I were proof of his reasoning.

Nesbitt sighs, takes a little road map of Mexico from his pocket. He unfolds it in front of Camado, says, "Where should we go?"

Camado stretches forward to look at it for a moment; he indicates vaguely an area near the Arizona border; he says, "Here."

"But isn't there a particular place?" Nesbitt says. "A name? Something specific?"

Camado shakes his head, no; he points, even more generically than before, without even putting his finger on the map. He says, "Just stay in this zone here."

"But what about the road you mentioned last night, the one that's all curves?" Nesbitt says. Obviously he's making an effort to remain calm and salvage what he can; he says, "Where's that?"

"Ah, I don't think you'd manage to find it," Camado says. He gesticulates, says: "The important thing is for Dru to get an idea of the landscape, the light, the vegetation, and so on."

Dru says, "Of course," looks at Nesbitt, who with a felt-tip pen draws a circle around the vague area on the map.

Camado stands up, says, "I must go. We'll talk as soon as you're back."

But Dru doesn't let him get away like this; he says we'll go upstairs with him.

We walk along the corridor and up the steps like three cops with a crook, Dru deliberately slowing the pace. He's cruel now; Camado keeps looking around, moving jerkily; every second we keep him here, he becomes more agitated. In the lobby he shakes hands with us all; he says, "Well, have a good trip, then." He tries to smile, but fails; he waves, and the wave also fails. He goes off a few paces, comes back, hands Dru the stick of power, says to him, "You keep it."

Dru accepts it automatically, before he realizes that Camado is at least thirty feet away by now. He is almost hopping, without looking back or slowing down, until he is outside the glass doors of the side entrance.

Then Dru twirls the stick of power like a vaudeville cane; he says, "All right. It seems to me we can go back to London now."

Nesbitt turns and looks at him, his eyes filled with genuine anguish; he says, "Don't you want to take a look, at least, at these places in Mexico? Now that you've come all this way?"

"We don't even know *which* places, Jack," Dru says, in his

definitive tone. He isn't the sort who, in situations like this, spares people's feelings.

Nesbitt moves to his other side, says, "Only two days, Dru. We'll come right back. Rather than give up completely."

"I can't," Dru says. He turns to look at a fairly sexy brunette, who walks past, followed by a porter with her baggage. He says, "I have a lot of things to do in London. I don't have time."

Nesbitt puts his hands in his pockets; he stares at the door where Camado went out. The abandoned film is in the air: a kind of vibration just below or just above the muffled sounds of the lobby. Some old ladies dressed in pink and apricot form a little group near the elevators; the cashier is behind his window with its gold bars; people are telephoning and approaching or coming away from conversations; they enter and exit. A voice over the loudspeakers says, "Mr. Resnik, Mr. Resnik, come to the Information Desk, please." The words are repeated two or three times before Dru recognizes his name and goes to the desk. One of the uniformed girls hands him a folded slip of paper; Dru opens it, holds it an inch or two from his eyes, turns to ask the girl something, looks at the note again. He comes slowly back toward me and Nesbitt. He shows it to us.

The regular print of the telegram says: IF YOU LEAVE THIS CONTINENT NOW NOTHING WILL EVER BE CLEAR WE ARE ASSISTING YOU.

I point to the hour of arrival marked in a square on the form; I say, "Eight-forty-five."

Dru and Nesbitt also look again. Nesbitt says, "How the hell did they know, two hours ago, what the situation would be at this moment? Before Camado had telephoned me or anything?"

We stand there in the lobby, with people going by on all sides, Nesbitt with the message form in his hand, Dru with the stick of power.

In the end Dru says, "Let's go to Mexico, goddammit."

We glide along

We glide along at more or less the same speed as the cars in the other lanes: passing, being passed. Nesbitt doesn't have to do much, just graze a button or two, adjust our course a little. There is almost no vibration, no need to brake or swerve suddenly, or step on the gas to avert trouble. The landscape is only a flat succession of squat buildings, yellow and white walls, billboards, motel signs at the edge of the traffic. There is no story behind any of the elements of the scene, no meaning beyond their obvious meaning.

I look at a Ferrari cabriolet on our left, with two stocky men in T-shirts and sunglasses. It's ridiculous to buy a four-hundred-horsepower car in this country, where the speed limit is fifty-five miles per hour. Nesbitt also turns a couple of times to look, and the two seem to look back at him. He says, "They're not following us, by any chance?"

Dru stops looking at the landscape; he says, "Them?"

We check them for five or six minutes: they move ahead, then flank us again, then drop behind; they change lanes, veer off. Nesbitt says, "Unless somebody's taken over from them."

I turn to look: it's hard to tell, with all these cars beside us and behind.

Nesbitt says, "Sorry, but I want to be sure." He takes the first exit, leaves the freeway; he pulls up in the parking lot of a Holiday Inn. He rolls down the window, says, "If there's anybody, we'll see him."

Dru says, "Who do you think it is? The CIA, like Camado says? They'd have to be very sophisticated to use such an unsophisticated style: notes under the door and sibylline statements written in a shaky hand."

Nesbitt sticks his head out, looks at the parking lot and the road. He says, "Anyway, I can't imagine what reason the CIA would have to prevent us making a picture."

"Hm," Dru says. "They might not want me to revive these stories of Camado's that deal with drugs and the occult and the Third World. But the idea really is ridiculous."

"Or else it could be the Mexican government," I say. I can't see any reason for the Mexican government's intervention, either; but at this point we're exploring the possibilities.

"Or else a rival sect, or some individual fanatic," Nesbitt says, making his contribution.

Dru says, "And whoever it is, they said they're assisting us."

We stay in the parking lot another couple of minutes, then Nesbitt starts the engine again, and we go back onto the freeway. The landscape tends to thin out, become flatter and flatter; the cars are more widely spaced. We turn to check from time to time, but it isn't much use.

Almost at sunset a jumbo jet comes down and lands just to our right; Nesbitt says, "San Diego."

Dru says, "We'll stop here." He plants his feet, stretches back.

Nesbitt exits as soon as he can, follows the signs for La Jolla. The road climbs and then descends toward the coast, toward the low sun over the line of the sea. We glide around the curves of the landscape and we are in the town, on a main street lined by Spanish-style buildings prettified with little arches and low white walls. There are people strolling in front of the shopwindows: middle-aged couples, young families; pretty girls chat with muscular characters at the doorways of cafés and ice-cream parlors. It seems a very pleasant place, after all these hours of looking at cars and overexposed landscapes.

We pass a building nobler than the others, a kind of governor's palace with garden and porch. Over the gate is written CARDINAL INN. Nesbitt checks Dru, says, "Shall we try here?" Dru says, "Yes, yes," opens his door before the car has actually stopped.

We cross the porch and enter a little lobby paneled in old polished wood. The furniture and the details of the decoration are twenties; on the windows of a small room higher up, the sunset glints. The manager behind the counter seems to date from the same period as the hotel; he makes a stiff little half-bow when he sees us. Nesbitt asks if he has three rooms for us. The manager shakes his head, says, "I'm afraid not, sir." He opens the ledger, says, "We're all reserved. I'm sorry." He turns the book toward Nesbitt, to show him it's the truth.

Nesbitt looks at the desk, says, "But . . ." He points a finger at the little row of names, says, "These are *us*. Nesbitt, Resnik, Hollis." Dru also sees them; he has a strange expression.

The manager turns the ledger around, looks at the names, looks at Nesbitt. He says, "I'm sorry. You didn't say you had made reservations."

"We didn't make reservations," Nesbitt says, a faint alarm in his eyes. He says, "We decided, just this moment, to turn in here." Dru rubs one hand over his neck.

The manager shakes his head, says, "I have reservations in these names."

"This is absurd," Nesbitt says. "I don't understand who can have done it. We didn't have the slightest idea we'd be coming here."

The manager gives him a hostile look, says, "Do you want the three rooms or not?"

"Yes, but it's absurd," Nesbitt says.

A porter carries our suitcases to the elevator; a girl in uniform slides the door shut and operates the switches. It's an old iron cage but well oiled, which goes down rather than up because the hotel descends from the street level to the sea. The porter leads us along a narrow corridor, over a floor that creaks beneath our feet. The building seems too fragile to have lasted so long; at this point, it must remain standing thanks to a delicate equilibrium.

The porter opens two doors, then says the third room is on the floor below. Dru looks at me and at Nesbitt, uncertain which of us he wants next to him. This isn't the sort of place where you feel like being very isolated, particularly now, with the purplish light coming through the windows. Finally Dru points to me; he says, "Maybe Dave could stay here and you could take the room downstairs, Jack." And he says, "Or vice versa." But Nesbitt is already following the porter along the hall.

The room is pleasant enough, though a bit cramped. I test the bed, press one knee on it: it seems flexible. From the window the ocean can be seen in the remaining light; a fire escape goes down against the rear façade. The system of pipes in the bathroom is exposed; there are heavy faucets with curved lines. I turn on the shower, let the water run.

I am under the too-hot spray, and there is a knock at the door. I wrap a bathrobe around me and go to open it.

Dru enters, goes straight to the window, comes back. He says, "They called me."

"Who?" I say.

"I don't know," he says. He goes back toward the window; he can't keep still. He says, "It must be the same people who wrote the messages, but it all makes less and less sense to me."

I ask him: "What did they say to you?" I feel ridiculous with this robe on, short and shrunk after being washed too many times.

Dru goes back to the door; he says, "Tell Jack to come up to the lobby; we have to talk this over." He goes out.

Nesbitt joins us with the face of one expecting the worst; he stumbles on the shallow steps leading up to the little room where Dru and I are. He says, "What did they say to you?"

"Nothing much," Dru says. "Welcome, and that they're assisting us."

"But did you figure out who the hell it might be?" Nesbitt says. "What sort of voice did he have?" A couple, their faces tautened after several lifts, are seated on a sofa to our right; in the lobby below there is little movement.

Dru says, "He had this strange tone, almost electronic, but

not exactly. With a mechanical cadence; but all the same, there seemed to be some kind of expression, underneath."

"It wasn't taped?" Nesbitt says.

"It didn't seem to be," Dru says. He looks at an ugly seascape on the wall, says, "But it lasted only a couple of seconds in all; it could have been taped."

Nesbitt takes a few steps on the parquet floor, says, "All right. Here we're dealing with an organization that clearly follows every single move we make, wherever we are. And they must be fairly professional, if they know our room numbers even before we do." He turns to look at a little family of three heading for the exit.

Dru says, "But, in your opinion, what are they aiming at?" He's not the least amused now; he runs a finger along the ridge of his nose.

"I don't know," Nesbitt says. "But I bet they have an eye on us at this very moment."

We go to the front desk, Nesbitt asks a girl there if she can remember the voice that called Dru. The girl says it didn't go through her; she asks the other operator, but the other operator doesn't know anything either. Nesbitt asks if anyone came and asked for us, or if anyone followed us when we checked in; the two girls shake their heads. They are ill at ease, they probably think we're mixed up in some kind of shady deal. The manager watches us from his desk; he follows us with his eyes as we go to the exit.

Outside, we walk along the slightly sloping pavement, we pass the local girls and boys, the couples, the weekending families, as shopwindow lights and street lamps come on one after the other. Nesbitt looks at the movement in the street, looks behind him; he says, "If we had at least an *idea* of who they are."

45

We go on for a few minutes, till we come to steps that lead down to a deluxe shopping center, constructed vertically like a little fake fishing village, with fake wooden cabins connected by decks that overlook a little fake square with a restaurant. We go down into the square, we sit at one of the tables. Nesbitt immediately asks the stolid-faced waiter if it isn't possible to find a better position, a better light; he names two or three wines and vintages that they don't have. I believe he needs to direct his dynamic energy somewhere; he feels lost if he can't take charge of something. He turns in his chair; for three hundred and sixty degrees he checks the people at the other tables. He says, "Sooner or later they'll have to show themselves."

We eat some fish with tasteless white flesh and a creamy almond sauce; we try to summarize the series of anonymous messages. We try dismantling them and putting them back together according to different keys, but it's futile. Dru doesn't say much; he drinks California Riesling and looks at a girl two tables farther on who smiles at him a couple of times. Nesbitt ventures hypotheses to explain Camado's sudden fright; he says, "It's *unbelievable,* him running away like that."

When Dru is tired, we leave. Instead of climbing the steps, we take a low street that curves down toward the ocean. The air is lighter and cleaner than in Los Angeles; there's the scent of flowers from carefully tended gardens. The moon is half-full, bright. We walk slowly in this little weekend paradise, with the film already lost, practically speaking, and no real reason for being here except for Nesbitt's insistence and Dru's curiosity.

Dru walks backward for a stretch, his hands in his pockets; he says, "Maybe it's just somebody who loathes my pictures and can't bear the thought of seeing another. Maybe he wants to wipe out all three of us, to eliminate the possibility for good and all."

"My God, Dru," Nesbitt says; he turns to look at the empty street behind us.

We follow the curve and go back to the main street, perhaps five hundred yards below the Cardinal Inn. There are still people on the sidewalks, but not many now; a few cars pass slowly. A tricycle with an awning comes up the slope, pedaled by a blonde girl, with a couple of elderly passengers. She stops outside a café, unloads them.

Nesbitt looks at Dru; he says, "Want to take a spin?"

"Oh, for God's sake!" Dru says, even though he continues to stare at the scene, intrigued.

Nesbitt signals across the street, shouts, "Hey!" The girl turns, pedals over to us. Tanned and athletic, not bad-looking, she wears white shorts and a white T-shirt with *Tricycab* written on it.

Nesbitt asks her if she can take all three of us. She weighs us a moment with a look, says, "No problem."

We sit in the back; the girl starts pedaling uphill; she stands on the pedals. Dru says to her, "Are you sure we don't weigh too much?" She says, "Absolutely not." Dru smiles, looks at her behind through the little cotton shorts, looks at the sidewalk that flows past. Nesbitt is propped on one elbow, as if he were being taken through some Oriental city.

The girl says, "Do you want to go anywhere special or just for a ride?" She tries to speak easily, but it's obvious she is forcing herself to the limit of her strength. I feel sorry for her; it's embarrassing to sit in the back like this.

Dru says, "Is there a place with good music?" He has this sadistic streak, from time to time.

"What kind of music? Medium or loud?" the girl says, now short of breath, pressing hard on the pedals.

"Loud, loud," Dru says; he asks me and Nesbitt if we're comfortable.

We go on for another five or six minutes, the hill no longer very steep, luckily, until we're beyond the margin of the Spanish-style downtown section. The girl turns into a lot where a number of cars are parked, outside a kind of rural dance hall. Loud music comes from inside: "Johnny B. Goode" in a slow, accentuated version.

The girl says, "Here you are," rubs one hand across her brow.

Dru says, "You were fantastic"; he asks her what her name is. She says Mary Ann; he says it's a beautiful name. He adopts his seducer's tone now, after making her toil uphill like a slave; he asks her if she doesn't want to come in and have a drink with us. She thinks it over for a second, says yes. She must have recognized him at the very start, because as we head for the door, she says to him, "You're Dru Resnik the director, aren't you?"

He says, "Aha," as if it were something incidental, without looking at her. At times I get mad, because things always go so smoothly for him with women, so *automatically*. You wear yourself out being sensitive and developing your good features and creating a manner, and you'll never have a hundredth part of the opportunities he has just because he's Dru Resnik.

Inside, there are people absorbing the noise, seated at little wooden tables in a big, foggy space. There's a dance floor and a stage where the group is playing, but no one's on it yet. The place is fairly primitive, no connection with the immaculate and phony town farther below.

We drink a couple of beers, look at the distant group. Dru

acts coy with Mary Ann the cyclist: he takes her hand and reads the palm, describes her character to her. She laughs, tilts her head; she says, "It's *true!*" Nesbitt and I don't have much to do, except to look away and drink beer.

The dancing starts on the floor; the singer raises her voice: "Okay, move it!" I get up; I say, "I'm going over to listen a bit."

Dru says, "You mean you can't hear enough where we are?" The fact is, he likes always to have an audience, and the possibility of disengagement, until he's absolutely sure.

Nesbitt stands up, too; he goes with me toward the dance floor. We look to see if there are some cute girls among the ones dancing now, but there don't seem to be any. We go to the bar; Nesbitt orders two bourbons, insists I drink one. He leans his back against the counter, drains the first glass, immediately asks for another. He's soon high, his eyes dulled. He says, "What about this movie? You think we'll manage to make it?"

"I don't know. That depends," I say. The music is loud; I can't hear his voice very well.

Nesbitt finishes his second drink, becomes more unsteady. He shouts, "It's *sure* to be a success. I don't have the *slightest* doubt."

I nod. At the hotel this morning, Camado looked as if he was running out in a fairly definitive way, not intending to come back to work on the film.

Nesbitt orders a third bourbon; he says, "Those bastards know this very well. That's why they're trying to get it away from me. But if they think they can scare me with a couple of anonymous messages, they've made a big mistake." He turns to look at Dru, who is now reading the cyclist's arm.

I point to the dance floor, signal him to come with me. We

pick our way through the people dancing until we are just below the stage. The singer moves back and forth on her spike heels; she yells, "Clap your hands! Stamp your feet!" The music isn't much, but at this volume it doesn't make a great deal of difference. I dance in the crowd, circle around looking for a girl. There's one, but she's dancing with a bodybuilder; she looks at me two or three times, but when I go toward her, she turns away. Nesbitt has also noticed her and is trying to get closer; he dances a few feet away from her, with a parody of a seducer's stare. He manages with a minimal movement of arms and legs, not very well coordinated. The music is so loud that you can't make anything of it here so close to the stage. I follow the rhythm, with the bass and the percussion hammering at my temples, the singer's voice as cutting as a chainsaw. Nesbitt goes back to the bar, knocks off another bourbon or two; every time I look at him, he seems more unsteady on his legs.

Then I'm dancing more or less by myself and a girl turns up in front of me, almost rubs against me. Her hair hangs over her forehead; she shakes it in every direction. She's short, quick in her movements, hopping and smiling a short distance from me; we proceed together to the same pounding beat. At a certain point she jumps and gives me a kiss on the mouth. She laughs, purses her lips again, wiggles, claps her hands over her head. She must be full of coke or amphetamines or God knows what; she's sweating and frenzied. I take a look at Nesbitt; he's dancing almost on *top* of the bodybuilder's girl. She smiles alternately at both, doesn't seem displeased. Nesbitt and the bodybuilder look at her in the same way; they accentuate their movements as if to force her to choose, they pretend not to see each other.

The little one grabs me by the sleeve, shouts something to me. I shout "Whaa?" at her. They are practically playing inside our heads; we have the amplifiers a few inches from our ears. "Your name?" she yells, as if she were yelling to some savage an island away. I yell my name two or three times before she can understand. She shouts hers at me; I shout back that I can't hear. She tries to reduce the distance still further, but in the flashing light she has a round, ugly little face with eyes like pinpoints. I pretend to understand, I nod my head, yes. The electric bass rasps like a diesel tractor engine, the traps beat inside my eardrums. I make a brief turn and I see the bodybuilder pushing Nesbitt away with a nasty look.

I shake off the little girl, I cut through the thick mob. The bodybuilder gives Nesbitt another push with both hands, shouts something at him, with the veins and muscles of his neck swelling. I try to take him by an arm, but he shakes me off, doesn't even look around. Nesbitt tilts back without falling; he approaches again, hangs on to the other guy, tugs at the man's shirt. The bodybuilder's girl looks around in alarm but doesn't do anything. The guy tries to twist free, loses a couple of buttons; he becomes more furious than ever, gives another shove to Nesbitt, who again flies backward, falls among the dancers, who move aside and then resume dancing in all the racket. I bend over to pull him up, but somebody twists my arm behind my back, lifts me bodily, pushes me toward the exit, flings me out the door without saying a word. A moment later, Nesbitt and the bodybuilder also come flying out, land beside me.

There we are, in the cold, dark night, among the parked cars. The bodybuilder's girl also comes out; all four of us look at one another, not knowing exactly what to do. The bodybuilder is maybe six feet tall, but as wide as me and Nesbitt put together. I say to him, "These are trying times for all . . . " He yells, "Go back to your own fucking country, you bastards!" He yells this chiefly out of a sense of duty, with a voice and face ill-suited to his body, probably weaker than he would like. His girl takes him by the arm, leads him to a car, limping on her spike heels.

Nesbitt says, "I *am* in my own fucking country, and I'm free to dance with anybody I want!" He leans against the Tricycab, attempts to catch his breath; he turns in the other direction and vomits. I pace back and forth in the parking lot; this is a stupid situation.

Dru and Mary Ann the cyclist come out, arm in arm, as if they were leaving a theater after a premiere. Dru looks at Nesbitt, still bent over in the darkness; he says, "What happened to you? We saw the fuss but it wasn't at all clear."

I explain to him what happened; he goes and gives Nesbitt a few slaps on the back, says to him: "How's everything, Jack? Feeling better?"

Nesbitt coughs, says, "I don't know."

We stand there among the cars for a few more minutes, as Dru plants kisses on Mary Ann's hands and Nesbitt tries to pull himself together; crude music comes in waves from the dance hall. Then Dru points to the Tricycab; he says to me: "Dave, would you kindly take over the driving? It's downhill all the way from here."

So I sit behind the handlebars, and they get into the back; I press down on the pedals to get this ridiculous cart out of the parking lot. It's true that once we're in the street, it isn't such hard work, but it's not exactly fantastic, pedaling home the master and his lady, on an evening like this. I'm also slightly nauseated from the noise and the alcohol; my head is throbbing. Nesbitt, in back, is very pale; he says two or three times, "I'm sorry, goddammit." There is a strip of neatly cropped grass running parallel to the sidewalk.

While she is in there

While she is in there fussing around and washing or putting on her makeup or looking in the mirror, the old wooden walls amplify the sounds of running water, the sighs of the pipes, the valves opening and closing. The atmosphere is disjointed, not fluid, as I had imagined; neither attraction nor isolation is sufficiently strong to prevail over the other. I'm sorry I went to the trouble to arrange this moment, even if the trouble wasn't great, and to make it inevitable, when it would have been so much better to come upon it by pure chance, without altering flows. And yet at least part of the attraction is in this imperfection of states, in the possibility of consequences difficult to remedy. All the real seducers I've known had an aura that protected their self-concentration, a diving bell of single-

minded intention, hermetically sealed at any depth, but I'm afraid you either have it or you don't from the start, and it's a bit late for me to think about it now. The voice on the telephone, too, was disjointed in intention just beneath the timbre of a Japanese science-fiction animated film, full of barely perceptible fragments of caution and self-consciousness about the words used. Not reassuring, all things considered, but I don't believe I need to be reassured at this moment. Mostly, I'd like to know what the game is, and why I'm in it, why I don't get myself out of it.

Her little tennis shoes, for cycling, are on the floor, one lying on its side, and they, too, are full of pathetic expectations, not durable and yet thoroughly used.

I have a headache

I have a headache and my ears are still buzzing from last night. I go into the bathroom to drink some water from the faucet, to get myself back into shape, to try to remember why I'm here.

At moments like this, my job isn't even a job, it's just letting yourself be dragged around by somebody else's vague ideas. There's no use intervening, or trying ideas of your own; you keep quiet and almost invisible until they ask something of you. I'm beginning to understand now that being in films means waiting, idle, off camera seventy percent of the time.

I go to the end of the corridor, step out into the garden, which slopes down to the ocean. It's nine o'clock; no guests are to be seen yet. Farther down there is a small oval pool.

An attendant finishes setting up umbrellas, then quickly climbs the path with steps, slips into the hotel. The air is transparent; in the distance below, a girl chasing a dog along the beach.

I go down to the pool, passing a white wooden hut with SAUNA written on one side and GYM on the other. On the gym side there is Dru working out on a Nautilus machine. He says to me, "How's it going?" He presses down the handlebar with sharp jabs, huffs and catches his breath again.

"Fine," I say. I sit on the exercise bike, pedal a bit, but I realize it could seem an allusion to Mary Ann last night; I get off.

He carries on for a few minutes, slides out, changes machines without stopping, does about twenty reps for the forearms. It's typical of him to maintain this frantic pace, as if he had to prove something.

I ask him, "Any more messages or calls?"

He looks at me for a moment, says, "No." He increases the weight, begins pulling the handles again. He must have regulated it at the limit of his strength: he jerks angrily, makes the metal ingots slam against one another. At the first pause he says to me, "Would you go wake up Jack? Otherwise, God knows how long he'll sleep."

I go up to Nesbitt's floor, knock a couple of times. He says, "Who is it?" in a hoarse voice.

"Dave," I say. It's nine-twenty on a Saturday morning; he has a right to be left in peace.

He comes to open the door a crack, looks at me. His eyes are puffy, his hair stands up almost straight on his head. He says, "What's happened?"

"Nothing," I say. "Dru told me to wake you up."

He motions me to enter, says, "I'll be ready in a minute."

I look out the window as he fishes stuff out of the suitcase and stumbles to the bathroom, and I feel sorry for him. The fact is that for Dru this is all material, sooner or later he'll use it in some film of his, and for me, whatever happens, it's better than staying in London without work. But for Nesbitt it's nothing but disaster, it's the loss of the film he's dreamed of making for years.

After a few minutes he comes out of the bathroom, all dressed, his cheeks pink from being shaved, his hair firmly combed back. With an effort he shifts his wallet and credit cards from one jacket to the other. He says, "I was thinking about it again for a moment, and I can't understand how we let ourselves fall for their game. The messages under the door and the obscure hints, now the phone calls." His dynamic energy has started flowing again inside him, fitfully; it's filling him with anger. He sets one foot on a stool, shines a shoe with a hotel cloth. He says, "What I mean is: I understand that a great director like Dru can be intrigued by the mysterious aspect of the situation; but still, we let ourselves be maneuvered like backward kids." He changes foot, says, "But I don't have the slightest intention of letting a bunch of cheap crooks get the better of me and screw me out of the movie."

"Naturally," I say. Now he's much less pathetic, moving confidently again; he's in the right.

He flings the cloth in a corner, says, "I don't give a shit who they are. This is a free country and I can drag the whole lot of them into court. I'll sue them for ten million dollars; we'll see if they still feel like sliding messages under doors."

We go out; he looks up and down the corridor. On the landing, he stares inquisitorially at a gay couple getting out of the elevator, until finally one of them stares back, irritated. Up in the lobby, Nesbitt goes straight to the desk, tells the girl on duty that he wants to talk with the manager. The manager arrives, already less than cordial, and says, "Yes?" Nesbitt says to him, "We want a list of all the guests for the past two days"; and he plants his hands on the desk.

The manager says, "I'm sorry, but that's impossible. Unless you're the police."

"We're not the police," Nesbitt says, "but you can rest assured that we'll call them if you don't give us the list."

The manager stiffens; he says, "May I ask what the problem is?" He is beginning to be alarmed, also because Nesbitt doesn't look at all like a poor weekend tourist or like some lunatic.

"We've been threatened," Nesbitt says. "We've received threatening messages from someone who has followed us to this hotel."

Now the manager is concerned; he glances to one side. One assistant is next to him, a deaf look on her face; the other is talking with a guest but she keeps her eye on us. The manager says, "What sort of messages?"

Dru comes out of the elevator with Mary Ann the cyclist; he comes to the desk. He says, "What is it?"

"I'm explaining to the manager about the threatening messages," Nesbitt says in his outraged tone.

"I don't think we could actually say they're threatening," Dru says. "The latest was a call wishing us good luck." He turns to look at Mary Ann, strokes her wrist.

The manager has a kind of tic that make him blink two or three times in a row; he says, "If you gentlemen wish, I can call the police immediately."

Dru smiles at him, says, "Thank you, but it hardly seems necessary."

Nesbitt is dismayed, says, "Now really, Dru . . . " Dru takes him by the arm, says to him, "Let's go have breakfast." Nesbitt tries to resist, refuses to budge; he says, "Wait . . ." Then he allows himself to be led away. The manager and his two assistants follow us with eyes of hatred, all lined up behind their counter of old dark wood.

We go out into the garden between the hotel and the road, sit at one of the many tables, all with umbrellas. Nesbitt remains standing; he says, "Dru, I don't know if you realize the situation." He turns to check the other guests: the weekend couples and the permanent couples, the couples on their honeymoon. He says, "They're *here*, goddammit, right now."

Mary Ann looks at him without understanding; she turns to Dru. Dru says, "Try to relax, Jack. They didn't sound dangerous, on the phone. And they said they're assisting us."

"And you think we should take them at their word?" Nesbitt says. He sits down, but in the most temporary sort of position, a three-quarters sit. He says, "Camado didn't seem all that relaxed, the last time we saw him."

A waiter comes over to pour coffee into our cups. Mary Ann orders toast and eggs and grapefruit juice, asks us what we're having, but nobody answers her; the waiter leaves. A couple is quarreling under the porch to our left; the woman strides furiously back to the hotel; the man goes as far as the gate, then changes his mind and runs after her.

The waiter comes back with toast and eggs and juice for everybody. Mary Ann spreads butter and honey with some hesitation; she tries to intercept Dru's gaze. She says to him, "Dru?"

Dru doesn't even look at her; he says to Nesbitt, "But at this point aren't you even curious to discover at least what they're aiming at? What they have in mind? Aren't you just a little curious?"

"No," Nesbitt says. He turns again, says, "Dru, for all we know, they could very well be a gang of *stranglers*."

Mary Ann swallows a morsel of toast, puts the rest on her plate. She no longer seems comfortable or interested in her breakfast; she looks at Dru.

Dru says, "The pair we saw in the hotel didn't look like stranglers, even though, to tell the truth, I haven't encountered many stranglers in my life and I don't know what they ought to look like. But there are three of us, after all, and we know how to defend ourselves, I hope."

Nesbitt says, "Dru, this is absurd. We should have informed the police the moment the first message came. Let's do it now, at least."

"Let's let them continue," Dru says. "Just a little longer."

Nesbitt shakes his head, looks at the cups and plates on the table. Mary Ann stares at all three of us, more and more uneasy. Dru remains concentrated on Nesbitt, seems to have lost interest in her completely. She finishes her grapefruit juice, looks at her watch a couple of times. She stands up, says: "I've got to run." She stands there expectantly. Dru looks at her as if he can't quite figure out who she is; he says "Ciao" to her; she goes off rapidly among the umbrellas. I feel like running after her myself; it's incredible how angry Dru makes me in situations like this.

Nesbitt looks away, says, "But . . . " There 's a busboy, who looks like an Indian, about ten yards away; he's staring at us with a barely perceptible smile. He shifts his gaze the moment he realizes we're looking at him; he vanishes beyond an umbrella. He reappears two seconds afterward near the hedge that separates the garden from the road; he fishes some knives and forks from a container, quickly polishes them with a cloth, and sets some tables. He moves mechanically from place to place, repeating the same, trained movements. He looks at us again, only an instant; I don't believe we'd notice if we weren't all so much on our guard.

Nesbitt starts to get up, says, "I'm going to talk with him."

"What do you want to say to him?" Dru says.

"I don't know. Ask him a couple of things," Nesbitt says. The busboy vanishes again among the tables; a second later he's on the porch, he enters the hotel. Nesbitt springs to his feet, follows him.

Dru and I remain seated, not saying anything; we look at the people eating breakfast, at the hedge, the porch. Then, as if synchronized, we get up; we also go inside.

Nesbitt is halfway along the corridor, near the door to the restaurant; he has the busboy nailed to the wall. From behind, we see his bulky form pressed against the much slimmer one in the black and white uniform. Dru grabs him by the shoulder; he says, "Jack! Have you gone crazy?"

"Leave me alone!" Nesbitt says; he shakes himself free, presses the busboy even harder against the wall. He says, "He just has to answer me, this bastard!"

Dru pulls him back bodily, says, "Cut it out, Jack! Calm down!" I lend a hand, too, to hold Nesbitt.

The busboy remains flattened against the wood of the wall; he breathes slowly. Nesbitt tries to assail him again; he yells, "He has to tell me why they've made us come here, this gang of sneaky bastards!"

We restrain him again, which isn't easy. Nesbitt has the physique of an ex-football player, well nourished and convinced he's right; rich and honest and exasperated.

Dru says to the busboy, "Try to forgive our friend. He's very tired." He turns and asks me, "How do you say tired in Spanish?"

"Cansado," I say.

"Cansado?" the busboy says in a faint voice; he slips to one side.

The manager arrives from the lobby, followed by two waiters. His expression has deteriorated; he says, "Now what's the problem?"

Dru says, "Nothing. We were just talking." He is still holding on to Nesbitt.

But Nesbitt remains with all his muscles tensed, his face flushed; he points to the busboy; he shouts, "We only wanted to know who the sneaky sons of bitches are who're paying this bastard!"

The manager struggles to maintain his control; he says, "Luis is an employee of this hotel, and if you have any complaints you should make them to me."

Dru says to him, "Now don't you get all upset, too."

We go to collect our luggage; we go outside. We wait on the sidewalk for the parking attendant to bring the car around; we are nervous now. Nesbitt looks upward, says, "Oh, shit."

We also look, Dru and I, and on a balcony across the street there is a life-size effigy of a hanged tiger, the noose held by the effigy of a monk. Dru looks, not moving, one hand on his hip. The effigies are realistic, sinister.

The car arrives; Nesbitt immediately grabs the attendant, says to him, "What's that stuff? Who put it there?"

The attendant has a stupid smile, says, "It's for tomorrow. We're really going to give those Tigers hell."

"What?" Dru says.

Nesbitt sighs. "They're the mascots of goddam baseball teams."

We remain for a few seconds on the sidewalk, then we slip

into the car, we look through the windows at the hanged tiger swaying in the still air, the hood of the faceless monk. Nesbitt backs up, shifts gear, drives slowly away. We look around again: none of us very convinced or reassured.

There are only a few dry bushes

There are only a few dry bushes in the broad gullies, and then
they disappear as well; there are only stones, stones bleached
by the violent light. It is a fragmented landscape shattered by
a giant pestle: flat spaces and hills and whole mountains of
gray shards. The road is empty before us and behind us, for
miles, as far as we can see.

Nesbitt suddenly slows down, says, "Did you see?"

"What?" Dru says.

Nesbitt points behind him, says, "There was a sign: We are
waiting for you."

"Are you sure?" Dru says.

"Of course I'm sure," Nesbitt says. "I'll go back and show
it to you." But as he is slowing down, there is a second sign:

WE ARE WAITING FOR YOU, written on a rock on the other side of the road. Nesbitt jams on the brakes.

We get out. The hot air hits us, almost makes us evaporate; with the air-conditioning and the smoked glass, we forgot we were in a desert.

We cross the road, shielding our brows with our hands. The rock with the sign seems neatly sliced, on the top of a pile of other rocks; the paint is fresh, it gleams white in the sun. We stand for maybe five minutes looking at it on the edge of the road, and there is no other car, no sound apart from the barely audible sizzle of the asphalt. We don't say anything, we hardly move. It's like being on another planet, not very habitable. In the end we get back into the car; we drive off.

After a couple of miles Nesbitt puts on the brakes again: there is a new sign, which says GET MOVING, WE ARE WAITING FOR YOU. But on a stone somewhat farther on there is also painted the form of a monk with a noose in his hand. Nesbitt says, "That goddam baseball game again."

And it's hard to understand whether it's only a coincidence or a parallel message or what. We go on through this endless expanse of stones.

The shards of the landscape crumble, are gradually pulverized; they blanch in waves of glassy sand that becomes more and more soft and shifting. Nesbitt is driving at a steady fifty-five, as if we had a police car right behind us. We listen to the hum of the engine, the rustle of the air-conditioning. Now there are real sand dunes, as in an African desert, except that instead of jolting over a dusty track we glide along this uniform ribbon of asphalt, not really *inside* the landscape, but slightly above it, or beside it.

We look at the dunes that flow past, and suddenly a little cloud of dust climbs up to a ridge, follows it, comes down. Another two or three appear in different places, and then there are dozens of sand clouds, each originating from a motorized tricycle running on taloned wheels. We can see the tiny, colored helmets of the riders, like marbles pursuing and overtaking one another and moving off along lines drawn by their own tracks. There is a campsite with trailers and pickup trucks and tents around which some human forms are moving. The trails of sand intersect in all directions until they create a dusty network that thins out. Then there is one, isolated, which runs almost parallel to us; it vanishes behind a wave of the landscape.

The dunes lose their cadence, turn gray, flatten. There are bushes; a billboard; other billboards, closer and closer together; a filling station; a garage and a supermarket and a Burger King; flat buildings and filling stations and supermarkets and neon signs and garages and asphalt courts, little houses with yards that become more and more substantial, then less; a filling station; two billboards; bushes and packed sand.

Nesbitt says, "Maybe we should drink something," but we are already well past the place.

We should be near the border, though there isn't the slightest indication of it. For some time the landscape has stopped changing; the road is straight and deserted; you could continue into infinity with no effort.

Nesbitt pulls off into a dusty field, unfolds his map. He looks outside for some reference point; he says, "Nobody comes this far east to go to Mexico. It's a hundred times more logical to go down from California, if you absolutely don't want to fly." Dru keeps quiet, his legs stretched out, his hands behind his head.

Nesbitt swings around, cautiously goes back; he stops every few minutes to check the map again. Finally there is a little sign: MEXICO. We follow it, down another road, and reach a small deserted town. Dru says, "We've been shut up in this coffin for *hours*." Nesbitt stops at an empty parking lot.

It's three in the afternoon, and the sun beats down with uniform violence; there isn't one dog to be seen, or a kid on a bike. It's a ghost town, with the windows shuttered and signs on the shops that say CLOSED, as if closed forever. Dru walks to the center of the road, looks around. Nesbitt tries to stay in the stripe of shadow along the walls, but he has to come out into the sun at the first intersection. Dru points to a bar on the other side of the road; we cross.

Inside, there isn't much light, the air is stagnant, not conditioned. There is a row of rough tables with two or three isolated customers; another customer is standing, leaning on the bar. Behind the bar a woman in a white apron is attaching a new keg of beer to the tap, slowly. They all seem on the point of falling asleep, annihilated by the void that's outside.

We sit at the last table in the rear. On the wall there are little strings hanging, attached to cowbells, obviously used to call for service in situations far more lively than this. The woman behind the bar raises her head, asks what we want. Dru says grapefruit juice. The woman looks at us as if we were making fun of her; the standing customer turns. Nesbitt says in a low voice, "I'm afraid the only thing you can have here is beer."

But Dru doesn't want to ask for it. It's one of his questions of principle, or perhaps he wants to put the woman and the customers to the test, drive the situation to extremes. He asks for three or four other drinks they obviously won't have in a place like this. The woman says, "We don't have any," looks at us with increasing hostility. Finally Dru asks for milk; she takes a carton from the refrigerator, fills three glasses, and puts them on a tray, comes and sets it in front of us without ceremony.

We drink the cold milk, look at some signs with jokes and old saws on the walls. Nesbitt perhaps is thinking about the dwindling chances of making the Camado film; he doesn't seem to be in a very good humor. Dru turns two or three times to stare at a man sitting at a table near ours. The man seems to be dozing, propped on his elbows, like the others, but no, on the contrary, he is writing or drawing something: he makes brief marks on a sheet of paper, then goes over them, one by one, with the greatest concentration. After a while he realizes we are observing him; he covers the paper with one hand. He looks like a young actor, a star gone to seed, haggard, ravaged for his age. He smiles; he's missing a couple of teeth.

Dru points to the paper the man's hiding; he asks, "What are you writing?"

The man slips it into a folder, carefully closes it. He says, "It's a plan."

"What kind of plan?" Dru says, with the vampire eyes he gets whenever he thinks he can pluck something interesting from life.

"For the reconstruction," the man says. He's wearing an old work shirt and pants all torn and patched; his feet are bare, black.

Dru is careful not to press him too hard; he gives him a few seconds, looks at the cowbells over our heads. He says, "What reconstruction?"

The man smiles again, not at us. His eyes seem gray, though you can't really tell in this place. He says, "When the cities blow up and the people run away and they don't have any place to go." He speaks in an automatic way, untouched by skepticism, like some kind of missionary.

Dru asks him, "When is this supposed to happen?" He seems to be trying to figure out if there is a connection with the messages; what interpretative key to use.

The gray-eyed man signals to the woman behind the bar; he says, "Another coffee."

The woman doesn't seem pleased—a coffee costs only twenty-five cents—but she brings the pot over all the same, fills his cup.

The gray-eyed man takes a sip, doesn't look us in the face. He says, "They've gone on building without considering the cardinal points and they've filled all the spaces that ought to have remained empty and used the wrong materials and the wrong colors and the wrong dimensions, and they've closed off every side until the people have become poisonous, and now there are *millions* of poisonous people, and when the cities and the houses blow up, if nobody makes a plan for the reconstruction, there won't be anyplace to go."

Now Dru is really intrigued; he's motionless, as he is on the set when an actor gets the tone right and goes beyond the lines given him, not following directions or predictable models. Nesbitt looks puzzled, with his half a glass of milk in hand. The woman behind the bar and the other customers are miles away.

The gray-eyed man scratches the back of one hand. We wait for him to go on, but he seems to consider the subject closed. Dru says to him, "How do you happen to be here?"

He shakes his head, says, "My wife tried to kill me three

times; they were the ones who talked her into it but she wanted to do it even before, on her own. Now she's a famous singer and you see her all the time on TV, but then she had longer hair, and she tried three times to poison me, so I had to come here. Now she lives on the thirty-fifth floor of a building, she records for CBS."

"What's your wife's name?" Nesbitt asks him.

The gray-eyed man stiffens, says, "They talked her into it, but she would of done it anyway, and she took our little girl, too, and now she lives on the thirty-fifth floor. All cities are wrong, they go on making engines and walls and radioactive steam and shutting off everything without a thought of the materials, and they attack space and smother it until it'll all blow up, and then people won't have a place to escape to if something isn't done in time." He presses his hands on the folder, he seems tired now, hostile.

Dru goes on staring at him, perhaps slightly disappointed by the circularity of his madness. Nesbitt looks at his watch, says in a low voice, "I think we should go, Dru."

Dru stands up, says to the gray-eyed man, "We have to go."

The man looks at us as if he doesn't understand.

Dru asks him, "Is there anything we can do?" He is still intrigued and looking for connections, hesitant.

The gray-eyed man seems to be thinking about the meaning of the question, seated with his cup of coffee in front of him, with Dru and me staring down at him from above, and Nesbitt anxiously looking toward the exit. Finally the man shakes his head.

We say "So long" to him, but he doesn't answer; he has already taken the papers from his folder again and gone back to making marks with his felt-tip pen.

Outside, the light is still violent, the town deserted.

Around four-thirty we cross the border. We're the only ones going in that direction; the customs men don't even look at us, they look at the car.

Then we're on the other side, in a town that seems to have been devastated by some catastrophe. The asphalt of the road is swollen and cracked, full of holes; the buildings are crumbling, with opaque windows, unhinged doors. There is dust everywhere; it rises in clouds as we pass. Barefoot children play on an intermittent sidewalk so high, it seems made to avoid sudden floods. The posters are all faded, torn.

Nesbitt drives slowly through what looks like the wreckage of an American town. Dru says, "Stop a minute." There is a little combo in front of a hardware store, and it's playing for *nobody*. Dru lowers the window: five men with sombreros on their heads, dark eyes and mustaches, big guitars slung over their shoulders. They are performing an ugly, sentimental, bogus song, addressing the road as if they were part of a scene staged for tourists, except there are no tourists here, and this place surely doesn't look as if it would draw any. We sit and watch them for about thirty seconds, from our black Mercedes, then Dru says, "Let's go. Otherwise they'll think we're talent scouts."

Nesbitt drives along, close to some buildings ruined and blackened by a fire or perhaps an explosion; he leaves the town, heads south. The landscape is the same as on the other side of the border, only the road is narrower and more unsure. Then the barren plain slowly changes color, becomes covered with yellow fields of corn, broken by paths and little clearings of packed earth where wrecked cars and pickup trucks are lying. There are peasants' huts, ditches, canals for irrigation.

Nesbitt says, "This doesn't look much like the places in Camado's books."

"No," Dru says. He looks at the cornfields; he says, "I don't know what a witch doctor could do around here."

Nesbitt pulls over, takes out the paper with Camado's vague indications, but this is the area, all right. He says, "Shit." He seems more disheartened than furious, like somebody who has just been sold a desert plot described as a forest. He says, "He sent us to the first insignificant place he could think of, just to get rid of us."

Dru shakes his head, says, "And all that stuff he told us about the road, the terrible curves, the unbearable sleepiness."

"I can't believe this," Nesbitt says. He drives on, looks to the left and right with barely controlled anguish.

We travel south for at least an hour, we change roads two or three times, we look for signals or surprises of some kind in the landscape. But there are only flat, cultivated fields and reddish earth, there is nothing particularly inspiring.

Nesbitt stops in a paved area, gets out, takes a furious turn around the car, rests his behind against the hood. Dru and I also get out, stretch our legs. Dru says, "Jack, let's not take it too hard."

"That's easy to say," Nesbitt says. He slams the flat of his hand on the heavy, black metal; he says, "If we at least understood what's happened, why Camado got scared or who these message people are exactly, what the hell they want. You must admit, it's not exactly a thrill to see everything go up in smoke and not be able to do a thing. Jesus."

"No, of course not," Dru says in a sympathetic tone.

All three of us stare at the expanse of corn, then we get back into the car; Nesbitt starts the engine again. We haven't even had anything to eat since this morning; I'm beginning to feel hungry.

Dru says, "Maybe the film would have turned out a flop and you'd have lost a pile of money."

"It would've been a *triumph*," Nesbitt says in a weary voice. "I'd bet my life on that."

We drive for another hour along various routes, then Nesbitt stops again, says, "Should we go back home?"

"Maybe we might as well," Dru says. He tilts his seat back, puts his feet on the dashboard.

At the first intersection Nesbitt turns north, follows the signs for Mexicali. We stop paying attention to what's outside; we let the landscape flow by like a TV documentary.

Dru starts telling us about when he shot his first films in Yugoslavia, the ways he invented to make them give him more film than he had been allotted. He says, "There was this official of the Academy of the Arts who was supposed to approve every script; his name was Ivo Kucharic; he had a kind of gray crew cut, little hamster eyes. He'd sit there behind his desk in an office with greenish walls and he'd tell you you had to cut or change or rewrite, as if in his files he had a perfect model for the sort of story yours should be. It's incredible the amount of *hatred* we lavished on him, all of us. But I believe it was a kind of nourishment for him; it didn't seem to harm him in the least."

"It must have been terrible," Nesbitt says.

"It was like being shut up in an old high school that's falling to pieces," Dru says. "You could be the diligent student or the student who created problems, but they were always student problems, no matter what. And we always had the idea that at the other end of the world we could make all the films we wanted, exactly the way we wanted. Total freedom of expression." He laughs, looks outside. He says, "It takes you a while to realize that making a film is like discovering a little spot you like while you're out taking a stroll, and so you decide to bring a whole busload of paying tourists there. At first you have to convince the owners of the bus, the ones who buy the fuel and pay the insurance and put air in the tires. You have to transfer your little mental stroll onto scale maps and attach photographs and explanations, guarantee the navigability of the roads and the beauty of the region, assure the right people that your original impressions are accessible and can be reproduced. And in the end, if you're not entirely worn out by all the friction, you can go back to the spot you liked so much and you can let it be invaded and trampled on and littered up."

Nesbitt says, "But it also depends on who the owner of the bus is, doesn't it? And who the tourists are."

"And who owns the road," Dru says.

Nesbitt turns down the air-conditioning, tries to avoid the potholes. We pass a ruined filling station, a donkey immobile in a field.

Dru says, "Do you also drive through a landscape sometimes and find your mood changes for no apparent reason?"

"Yes," Nesbitt says.

"Sometimes," I say.

Dru says, "It's a kind of electromagnetic radiation that every place gives off, in a different way. You go by fast, sealed in your car, with the windows carefully closed, and in a few seconds you're depressed, on the brink of suicide."

Nesbitt looks away, accelerates.

Dru says, "When I was living in Italy, I bought myself a Ferrari, to drive faster, but it wasn't much use. The whole country is so torn and dented and shattered, the radiations *drill* into you. You can't drive a mile without seeing an excavation, a hill that's been decapitated or a concrete wall or an industrial shed or a row of monstrous buildings right on the road, or a furniture store in a lake of asphalt, or a bunker-supermarket that stretches for a thousand feet. I drove that sort of pimp's car always over the speed limit, I must have been fined two hundred times."

"They have those incredible engines," Nesbitt says.

Dru scratches his knee, says, "People don't realize how dangerous negative landscapes can be. If you cross them without any kind of shielding, on a motorcycle, for example, they can even destroy you. I'm sure there are people who are dissolved, never found again. They find only the motorcycle and can't understand what happened. And imagine what it must be like for the people who *live* there."

Nesbitt looks at him, trying to figure out if he's joking.

Dru says, "But it's complicated. Just because a place isn't devastated, it doesn't necessarily transmit positive radiations. There are landscapes, seemingly natural, that fill you with shadow or with sleep or with a feeling of guilt. And stupid landscapes, limited, carefully constructed from nothing, or even completely uninhabitable, and yet they reassure you. It's hard to say, until you're inside one."

Houses can also be depressing, I would like to add. I think of my disgusting kitchen in London; there must be some electromagnetic radiation there, too.

Then it's already sunset and we're in Mexicali. We arrive without realizing it: one minute we're among cornfields in the still-hot light, and the next minute on an enormous, jolting avenue among streams of old cars and pickup trucks that jerk and grate and saturate the air with their stink. We bounce around a kind of square with a statue in the center, of somebody reclining on an outcrop of rock facing north, and we let ourselves be carried along by the traffic among insane constructions and street lamps that begin to turn on and the honking and exhaust and creaks and explosions and fumes that rise over the yellowish horizon veined with sepia and dirty purple streaks.

Nesbitt drives tensely; he has to swerve and brake every two seconds, duck cars that cut in front of us or try to force us out of our lane or push us forward or drive us back. The buildings on either side increase in girth, covered with signs and display windows and flashing neon and steady neon. The river of traffic slows down until it stops; it goes forward then in fits and starts. There are shabby little supermarkets with prices in red on the windows, theaters showing karate movies and soft porn, clothing stores, hamburger or taco joints, liquor shops, cars parked sideways across the pavement, or in double or triple rows into the middle of the street. There are people who are dealing at the gas stations or outside the doorways of bars, under crumbling arcades: young whores with dyed and teased hair, dangerous men gesticulating in little groups, trading jokes and insults in the riot of noises and lights and mechanical movement. It is a kind of postatomic metropolis put together with the ruins of the metropolis that had been there before, with no concern other than to continue somehow the dealing and the entertaining and making people enter and exit containers for people.

Dru is fascinated by the wreckage; he observes the outline of a building that seems on the verge of collapsing into the street; the movement outside a boot shop, outside a Kentucky Fried Chicken with cracked panes. He says, "Let's stop a minute." Nesbitt looks at him in alarm, he looks outside; he double-parks just beyond a gallery where some characters in black leather jackets are sketching some dance steps. He says, "I don't know if it's a good idea, Dru."

Dru opens the door, says, "Stay here, if you want. Dave and I will just stroll for a moment."

I get out, even though I'd be quite happy to wait in the car. Nesbitt looks really worried; he turns to check the street. The air smells of carbon dioxide and spun sugar and gas and burned rubber and barber's perfume, so dense it's hard to breathe. Dru walks past a little group of smokers, who turn to look, then past a shop that sells wedding dresses, its windows crowded with dummies. There is a boy sitting on a big motorcycle, who guns the engine for two or three observers; people listening to disco music in a car with its windows rolled down; a girl crying and yelling and pulling the hair of a fatter woman with her back to the wall. There are rapid signals from one side of the street to the other, faces that peep out and draw back at doors and entries, whispers, laughter, clicks, hums, flashes, puffs, sudden gusts of new odors, sweetish and sharp. I try to keep up with Dru, my heart pounding as if I were in the midst of an automobile accident. We walk rapidly, set one foot in the traffic of vehicles, one in the traffic of people, and we are increasingly besieged, on all sides, by looks and movements and noises; we edge forward, expecting at any moment a blow or a loud report, until we have trouble just swallowing, and even Dru understands. We turn and head back quickly, almost running, until we find the street and the car.

Nesbitt is clutching the wheel under the eyes of a trio of men with glistening hair, who from the sidewalk seem to be weighing the possibilities of dismantling the Mercedes and selling its parts. He unlocks the doors as soon as he sees us, locks them again the moment we're inside, and pulls out quickly into the traffic. It is night, too: the neon of the shopwindows casts blue and red glints on the damp asphalt, on the backs and windows of the cars that proceed with effort in the air full of fumes.

Nesbitt follows the signs for the border, but it takes us half an hour to get there, though it's less than a mile away. We are tense and silent while waiting in line, we don't take a deep breath until we are past the checkpoint and in the United States, on the straight, broad road leading north.

Dru says, "Do you feel like going on, all the way to Los Angeles?"

Nesbitt lets me have the wheel only when he's on the point of collapsing; he explains to me ten times how the controls work. Dru looks out, even though there's not much to see apart from the darkness. Nesbitt closes his eyes; he reopens them, pretends not to have closed them at all. He doesn't have much faith in my driving; he says, "Maybe just a bit slower, Dave." I accelerate the moment he dozes off again.

We stop at a kind of empty aquarium, which is a bar. There are two pale waitresses and a customer with a depressed look, slumped at a table. We have a couple of coffees each, walk back and forth on the white tiles. One of the waitresses starts talking to Dru, and without having the slightest idea who he is, she says she wants to be an actress. She strikes a couple of poses as demonstration: with her hands on her hips and her chin raised, she flutters her eyelids. But she must not believe in the whole thing much herself, because she next lets out a shrill laugh, in the circular room, all glass.

We are again among the flat suburbs; the opalescent light quickly turns yellow. Then the sun is high, and we're in Anaheim among more and more cars; we're almost in Beverly Hills; at the driveway of the hotel.

We go and collect the keys to our rooms; Dru asks if there have been any calls or messages. The man on duty at the desk says no; he seems amazed to see us so disheveled and untidy compared with what we were two days ago. We go off a few steps and look at one another, and suddenly the situation seems incredibly sad and futile.

Dru taps his key on the palm of his hand, says: "I don't know what we were expecting, after all. To find a script, all ready and bound, in some cornfield, a hundred times better than all Camado's books put together, and without even having to ask anybody for the rights?" He turns toward Nesbitt; he says to him, "What were we expecting?"

Nesbitt doesn't answer; he looks down.

I don't know what I was expecting, either. Maybe to tag along in this vague well-being for another month. I don't know. It's true that the story wasn't mine, but I was in it as much as Dru and Nesbitt; I wasn't in any hurry for it to end.

Nesbitt says, "Will you two go back to London, then?"

"Aha," Dru says.

If he would agree to trade house and work and prospects, I'd even be willing to take on Verena and all the probable sentimental and organizational and fiscal headaches he's anticipating now; willing to take on the disappointment that is now making him chew his lip.

He says to Nesbitt, "Can you make reservations on the first flight tomorrow?"

"Of course," Nesbitt says, in the steadiest tone he can muster.

Dru says, "We'll meet around seven"; he slips into the elevator without even waiting for me.

Maybe I had begun

*Maybe I had begun really to believe there was a story behind
those messages, like something out of a little TV thriller. With
the coincidences and the places and the moving around and
the sounds, I was nearly convinced that I had only to follow
a trail from contact to contact, gathering material effortlessly,
without waits or slow distillations or sublimations or transfer-
rals or excavations or thefts of sensations. I would gladly have
run a few risks in exchange. Instead, this poor mythomaniac
or little group of mythomaniacs has become afraid of discovery,
or they've run out of money, or, as happens with mythomaniacs, they've tired of the whole thing and are now concen-
trating on something else with the same intensity, and we've
been left high and dry like three helpless fish, unable even to*

take it with a sense of humor. If it hadn't been for me, I don't think Dave or Jack would have gone along with the game this far. They're not exactly filled with admiration for the way I fell for it. It's pathetic how you can endow the first anonymous voice with all the depth and allusions and strange angles you'd like to find; it's like convincing yourself that the tricks of a prestidigitator are magic or the special effects of a film are genuine catastrophes or a woman you meet in the most casual way is the woman of your life. Without realizing it, you make little opaque curtains and project on them your most confused and remote desires, you make your desires attainable for a moment. And probably, each time, there are identifiable motives behind these flashes of unthinking receptivity; if I wanted to, I could retrace my steps to the story I was expecting to find preestablished by others, and maybe I would discover a film much more interesting and profound than those I've made so far. Or maybe, on the contrary, it would be confused and vacillating and impossible to make, or, worse, organized with irreparable coherence around a single idea, without the slightest room for a doubt or a shadow or an ironic touch. Maybe I would do well to feel relieved, instead of brooding so much on this.

I go to Dru's room

I go to Dru's room around seven. He and Nesbitt are there, standing, dressed elegantly for the evening; only their lack of tension shows how disappointed they are. Nesbitt says to me, "Camado's disappeared. Kate, Maribel, his agent, nobody has any idea where he is. Vanished." He makes a gesture meaning vanished.

"You could tell from his behavior, when he left," Dru says. He opens the closet, takes out the stick of power Camado gave him in the lobby. He weighs it in his hands, runs his fingers over the smooth wood; he puts it back in the closet. He says, "Let's try at least to do something amusing this evening. Not stay shut up in here, moaning."

"Sure," Nesbitt says. He takes two or three steps, says, "What would you like to do?"

"Anything except see people I already know," Dru says in his spoiled superstar tone.

Nesbitt hesitates a moment, says, "If you like, I could call my girl and see if she has any ideas. She'd love to meet you."

"Call her," Dru says. "Tell her to bring along a cute friend."

Nesbitt telephones immediately; he speaks in a low voice, hunched over the receiver.

Dru says to him, "And her friend," signaling insistently from the other side of the room.

Nesbitt tells his girl. Now, I'm not all that eager to be the chauffeur of the situation; I say, "Maybe *two* cute friends."

Nesbitt turns and looks at Dru for confirmation. Dru says, "No, no, one's enough. We're not going to play the dating game."

I don't make an issue of it; I guessed this. He has this tendency always to arrange things in such a way that you're never completely satisfied or self-sufficient when you're dealing with him. He likes to keep you in a state of constant slight deprivation.

So Nesbitt repeats "No, one's enough" to his girl, who could probably have brought along ten cute friends without any problem. He hangs up, says, "We'll pick them up at eight."

"Wonderful," Dru says, rummaging in a drawer.

I'd like to give that piece of furniture a kick, go off on my own, tell them all to go to hell.

Nesbitt calls a restaurant and makes a reservation, then we go down to the bar, drink white wine without being thirsty, and venture more pointless conjectures about who wrote the messages and why they stopped and where the hell Camado could have gone. At twenty to eight we go out.

Seated in the back seat of the car, I sniff their toilet waters, equally expensive; I look at the equally perfect tailoring of their blue jackets. Mine is secondhand and the sleeves are too short; it can pass muster only in semidarkness. But I'm afraid it's clear that, jacket or no jacket, I am the assistant. I wonder if I can pass myself off as a young associate producer or scriptwriter. Maybe a scriptwriter, if Dru or Nesbitt doesn't give me away.

Nesbitt drives through West Hollywood; he stops in front of a little white house with a hedge around it. He jumps out, says, "I'll be right back."

Dru looks at the little house and the little garden in the row of little houses and little gardens; Nesbitt opens the gate and runs the ten feet of front walk, knocks at the door. Dru says, "It's *Walt Disney,* only shabbier."

Nesbitt's girl appears, kisses him quickly, and comes immediately to the car. Dru and I get out; Nesbitt does the introductions, says, "Elaine Neals, Dru Resnik." She's cute in a showy way, with her carefully set blond hair, blue eyes, slim waist, long legs; she's wearing a tight black skirt and a black jacket, a little black hat with a veil. I shake hands with her; she looks at me with interested eyes until Dru says to her, "My assistant." Her interest dissolves at once; she says "Hi" without looking at me again.

She sits in front, twisted around, her arm along the back of the seat, addressing only Dru. Nesbitt drives to the other girl's house even more slowly than before; all his concentration is on his right.

Elaine talks about herself as if she had at her disposal only a limited number of minutes to present her interesting points. She says, "I'm a dancer in the West Round Ballet, which is directed by Miles Ninescu; but actually I believe I'm at a turning point in my career now, and I've decided to dedicate myself much more to the movies, though I don't want to grab the first part they offer me, I'd rather wait until I find something that suits my potential, because the easiest thing is to get off to a bad start and then nobody has the slightest interest in you. I think I have some important points in my favor, since there aren't many actresses around who *really* know how to dance and move well, *and* act."

"That's right," Dru says, having already formed, I believe, a precise picture of her.

Nesbitt is tense; he fiddles with the air-conditioning.

Elaine resumes at once, taking a different tack, without slowing the pace. She turns her head, displays her perfect profile, says, "I'm also kind of parapsychological; it's something I've had since childhood, and I've had simply *hundreds* of experiences that can't be explained, like contacts over long distances and transtemporal images and premonitions. For example, the night before the shuttle exploded in 1986 I dreamed about a great flash of light in the sky and this streak of white smoke exactly like we saw the next day on TV, when it all really happened. I felt terribly guilty then, because I thought I should have warned somebody, but apart from the fact that nobody would have believed me, I wasn't able to figure out what the dream meant; I just had this image, very vivid and clear."

"Incredible," Dru says, overwhelmed by all these words.

"What's the number?" Nesbitt says, to stop her.

But Elaine stops anyway, as if she had used up her allotted time. She makes a couple of gestures to indicate how far along the street.

We all get out; Elaine buzzes. The building is a small, modern condominium, three or four cubes connected by short flights of steps. Elaine says, "Rickie and I met in New

85

York because we worked with the same photographer." She looks at the condominium; she doesn't hunt for further subjects.

Rickie emerges from one of the doors and comes down the steps; she smiles at us long before reaching the gate. She's more or less the same height as Elaine and just as blond and showy, but her lines are rounder and softer, her hair is shorter, and she is dressed in white. She also concentrates immediately on Dru; she says to him, "I've always been a fan of yours."

Then, seated in the back between me and Dru as Nesbitt drives to the restaurant, she begins to swamp us with information about herself. She says she works for a company that distributes foreign films, but really she wants to be an actress, though she knows quite well that parts suited to a personality like hers are few and far between, and the casting of films is all in the hands of a mafia of three or four agents who deal directly with the producers and none of the new directors have enough clout to make their own choices, but she plans to go along with the game and have a try anyhow because she has a few aces up her sleeve, and she's not some poor hopeful kid, she has other fish to fry. She says she's been to Paris lots of times; and she hints that she had an affair with Gerlais, the French director. She speaks in a strange didactic tone which she must have learned in order to communicate with him, and this is probably the tone she uses with any foreigner, even English-speaking ones: every word accentuated and accompanied by complementary facial expressions and illustrative gestures. Dru seems amused; he smiles. Elaine, up front, is quiet, leaving Rickie the same space she had for her own self-introduction.

In the parking lot of the restaurant the two girls walk

ahead, arm in arm, on their high heels; Dru and Nesbitt follow in their blue jackets. I keep a few paces behind, really like a chauffeur.

The manager or proprietor wears an Italian suit with over-padded shoulders; he has glistening hair; he recognizes Dru at once; with little, controlled smiles he leads us to a table. There is just one big room full of rich and noisy people. Nesbitt looks around; he says to Dru, "Maybe you'd have preferred a quieter place. . . ."

But Dru doesn't even answer; he is already studying how to seat us. He takes the head of the table, puts Elaine on his right and Rickie on his left, Nesbitt and me at the extremes, so he has two girls for himself, leaving only half a girl to each of us. The two girls exchange looks, settle in the chairs, erect and prim. It's odd to see them facing each other like this, one dressed in black and the other in white, both blond and showy and magnetized by Dru in the same way.

Dru orders French champagne and oysters and Iranian caviar, everything on the menu that costs the most and makes the greatest display. He suggests delicacies to Elaine and Rickie, incites the two of them. He lowers his voice, makes cruel remarks about the people at the other tables. The two girls are ecstatic: they bow their heads, pretending to be indifferent, when the waiter moves around them to pour the wine in their glasses.

Nesbitt forces himself to interject a remark here and there, but he hasn't a chance of gaining attention for long. Dru lets him speak as support or counterpoint, when needed; then he interrupts a sentence, leads the conversation off in the direction he likes. He manages never to allow a gap in interest: he exploits my frustrations and Nesbitt's, from our outer edge, to make the atmosphere more intense. This is why he didn't want a third girl: he knows too well the principle of magnetic fields.

He tells about a time, years ago, when he was trapped in a hotel in Marseilles after the Italian producer had decamped and the hotel owner had decided to hold the whole troupe hostage. He narrates a couple of awkward or humiliating episodes in the sentimental life of some big American actors who have worked with him; he describes a couple of archipelagos in the Pacific; he compares islands as if he found nothing extraordinary about any of them. He shifts his gaze constantly, speaks in the tone of someone unwilling to guarantee he'll finish what he's saying. The waiters come and go with individual filets of fish and minimalist salads; the girls are so captivated, they don't even notice what they have on their plates. Nesbitt and I might as well be at another table.

Then Dru becomes fed up with this role of entertainer; he leaves the field to the girls, who quickly fill it with semiesoteric discussion, or, alternately, with much more ordinary subjects. It's amazing how they manage to talk with total concentration about ESP and astral influences and predestination, and then engulf us a moment later in details about cars and rock singers and exercise machines and diet problems, giggling and winking and waving their hands frivolously. It's as if they had two gears to choose from.

At a certain point a woman of about fifty rises from a nearby table and comes straight over to us, stops in front of Dru, swaying.

Dru looks up at her, tries to figure out if she's drunk or mentally unstable or what.

The woman runs her fingers through her hair, with its mèches. She's all dressed up, in high fashion, with a platinum-and-diamond watch, a porcine nose. She says, "I just wanted you to know I admire you very much and I've seen all your films four times."

Dru says in a lowered voice, "Very kind of you," as if he were thanking her for a note of condolence. I don't believe he ever feels entirely at his ease here in America, entirely sure about what lies behind what.

The woman dries the corners of her eyes, makes a faint bow, and goes back to her table. Here and there, other faces in the room have turned to follow the scene, but in a carefully disguised way. Rickie and Elaine seem tremulous, like two worshipers near a saint at the moment he works a miracle.

Dru says, "Maybe we can leave," and he's on his feet before anyone can express disagreement.

Outside, in the parking lot, he says to me, "You sit up front," and he slips in the back between Elaine and Rickie. He puts an arm around each, distributes compliments in a low voice, stimulates giggles and compliments in return. Nesbitt drives nervously: he almost sideswipes another car as he turns, he brakes in the nick of time at the first traffic light.

Dru says to him, "Well, Jack? Where are you going to take us?" He has a kind of Caligula tone now, sprawled in the back between the chirping girls.

"Wherever you like," Nesbitt says; he's trying to check in the rearview mirror.

Dru says, "Let's go to some decadent place. The most decadent place you know."

We're gliding along Sunset, among the billboards and the neon signs, the headlights and red taillights of the other cars. Nesbitt points to a two-story building all aglow on the other side of the street; he says, "Bako's is pretty decadent."

"Come off it," Rickie says. "Dru said he wants somewhere

decadent." She puts corners on her vowels, makes them come out three-dimensional.

Dru says to her in a whisper, "You know? You have an extraordinary way of speaking." More chirping follows.

"Hot Line?" Nesbitt says, trying to maintain contact.

"My God, that's about as decadent as the six o'clock news," Rickie says, making Dru laugh.

Elaine says, "I know a place. Turn west at the second corner."

Nesbitt takes a right, follows Elaine's directions. Every time, she keeps on snickering with Dru until we're three-quarters of the way past the intersection, then looks out at the last minute and cries "Left, left!" or "The other way!" Nesbitt brakes, the cars behind us have to brake; he says, "Maybe give me a few inches' warning, eh?"

As soon as we're past a low box of a building, Elaine says "Stop, stop" and opens the door. Nesbitt manages to take her by the arm as we cross the street, give her a kiss before we reach the other side. She flashes him a quick smile of reassurance, but the moment we go through the door, she's clinging to Dru again.

We move along an angled tunnel and we're in a big room, semi-Western style, with a rough wood floor and dim lights, disco music at medium-low volume. There are many little tables empty; the people are seated at the end, in the gloom, beside a raised runway that connects three circular platforms. There are no sounds above or below the throb of the music.

We follow Elaine, go and sit along a free stretch of the runway. The runway and the circular platforms are of white, semiopaque plastic, illuminated by neon from below. A girl with big eyeglasses comes forward on the catwalk; she slips off a skimpy diaphanous robe, drops it to the floor. Bedraggled, pale, she moves with a parody of sensuality, looking vaguely at the watchers seated below in the shadows. She walks in slow motion, stops, goes back a few steps, heads again for the platform. She slips off a diaphanous powder-blue bra, sways her flabby breasts, smiles emptily. When she reaches the circular platform, she spins around a couple of times, slips off the diaphanous blue panties. She lowers her body as if doing a balancing act, sits on the luminous plastic, leans back on her elbows; she parts her legs and raises them, turns slowly, with her glasses—a kindergarten teacher's glasses—refracting the light.

The watchers don't say anything, don't move; they stare, perfectly serious, between the girl's legs. They are almost all Japanese, some with their arms folded, others bent forward to be as close as possible. Every so often, one of them puts a dollar bill on the edge of the runway; the girl stops rotating for a moment, pauses, facing him.

We are also watching silently, and it's like being underwater. The other two girls, on the more distant platforms, make the same regular movements; the other watchers are immobile and absorbed in the same way. A sluttish waitress passes close to us a couple of times with a tray of soft drinks; we signal no to her. Elaine and Rickie exchange forced smiles and also smile at Dru, but nobody is amused much. It seems hard to move; we are entangled in the gloom.

The girl on our platform stands up, collects her diaphanous bra and panties and robe, puts them on again with no attempt at erotic grace; she resumes moving in the direction of the next platform, with the same walk she used when she came our way. The watchers follow her to a certain point and then turn in the other direction; they watch another girl, who now arrives, waggling her hips like the first one. The music is always the same, without discernible variation, based on a muffled rhythm. Dru looks a couple of times toward the exit, with the eyes of someone who feels trapped. Elaine says, "Shall we go?"

We leave, we start breathing outside, on the pavement. Rickie says, "Well," does a parody of the stripper's walk. Nobody laughs. Nesbitt says to Elaine, "How the hell did you know about a place like that?"

She turns to Dru, says, "I'm sorry. It was the most decadent I could think of."

We stand another few minutes with our backs to the wall, looking at the sparse nighttime traffic, then we cross the street, get into the car. Dru sits silently between the two girls; he seems depressed. But Rickie is still full of energy; she tries to recover the atmosphere of when we came out of the restaurant; she says, "Don't panic, everybody; it's only midnight. Let's think of something else."

Nesbitt is leaning on the wheel; he says, "Maybe Dru's tired."

"No, no," Dru says in a tired voice.

"I've got it!" Rickie says. "I know where we should go."

Dru says, "Let's give it a try." Nesbitt starts the car.

We cross the city toward the northwest at a steady speed. Elaine takes a white quartz crystal from her purse; she says her psychic gave it to her as protection against negative influences. Rickie has an almost identical stone in her jacket pocket, attached to a little chain. Dru puts them side by side, looks at them in the scant, flickering light. Elaine says, "It's not the same psychic, though."

We go past dark side streets, past lots illuminated by floodlights. After a while only Hispanics are to be seen, standing in little groups at the street corners or pressed around a car, leaning against a wall in quarreling pairs. Dru says, "Is it much farther?"

Rickie says, "Two more minutes, Dru; this is a big town."

Finally we stop in a parking lot full of broken-down old cars and pickups; we walk along the side of a big industrial shed that has some murales, but they're incomprehensible when seen this close.

The ticket seller is sealed in a little glass bunker; he waits until Nesbitt has slipped some money through a slit before he presses a button that makes the tickets come out. Without looking at us, an attendant tears them as we go through a heavy curtain.

Inside, the place is full of noise, voices, movement, and the eyes of hundreds of men crammed together: hoarse shouts, teeth bared, fingers flashing signals, whistles. A woman with elaborately teased hair is yelling like a lunatic into a microphone, conducting a kind of auction, though it's not clear what's being auctioned: her words disappear among thousands of other sounds. We make our way through the confusion, to some free seats at the edge of a boxing ring filled with mud. The men look around; they stare at Elaine and Rickie. Nesbitt clasps Elaine's arm, trying to shield her from this attention.

But the men have already stopped looking at her; all eyes are trained on a girl in a fake leopardskin costume, who passes through the mob followed by a stocky boy with a wooden box in his hand and a sign with $1 written on one side and $2 on the other. The girl pauses after every few steps; she inspires waves of laughter, shifting of seats, raising of hands. The boy moves on his short legs with an almost pathological elasticity, points to the hands in the order they are raised. The girl goes and snatches the dollars held out to her, passes them to the boy, who sticks them into the box; she grabs the men by the chin or by the nape and kisses them on the mouth, then immediately shoves them back. She wheels around like a real leopard when somebody pinches her behind; she spits, screams obscenities in a hoarse voice, responding to the shouts of the men.

Dru says, "My God," in a half-whisper. Rickie looks at us to make sure we have grasped the essential mechanism of what's going on; she points to a second kisser, much younger and prettier, in a beauty queen's dress with bare legs, pink shoes with high heels. The boy following her is sturdier than the other, almost a bodyguard. They pass close by us, and she seems completely impervious to what she's doing; she chews gum without the slightest trace of expression, genuine or simulated, on her face. She moves around with her smooth, Miss Oklahoma manner, kisses the mouths of the frenzied and sweating Hispanics as if she were performing some completely ordinary task. The boy bodyguard is directly behind her, making sure nobody reaches for her or tries to prolong the kiss more than usual. The two-dollar kiss also lasts less than a second. The men try to act as coarse and sniggering as they can; they gesticulate and yell and urge one another on, but as soon as the girl takes the money from their hands, they seem vulnerable for a moment, become serious and motionless as she kisses them and shoves them away. They look at her, dazed, as she moves off; it takes them a good ten seconds to summon up a smile or a vulgar remark.

Then the first girl, in the leopard costume, comes and leans on the ropes of the ring, takes a deep breath, shouts a few more insults left and right, until a pale, thin girl arrives. The first girl immediately grabs her by the hair and drags her into the ring, into the mud, and starts pretending to strangle her while the woman with the teased hairdo and the microphone resumes yelling something. Now it's clear why the seats facing the ring are empty: the mud spatters everywhere, along with the announcer's spit. We shift our seats back, but it isn't much use; we get up, remain standing for a few minutes to watch, then head for the exit among the noisy, overheated men, who vibrate, sitting almost on top of one another.

Nesbitt takes us back across the city; nobody says anything. The streets are almost empty; a few cars glide by in the livid light. We are undone by the Mexican trip and by the evening; we are destroyed.

Nesbitt stops outside Rickie's gate. Dru says, "Good," in a conclusive tone.

Rickie hesitates before getting out, says, "Why don't you come up for a few minutes? I'd like to show you a little videobook of mine. A little film of stills."

"I'm afraid we're in rather bad shape," Dru says; he tries to make her out in the light of the street lamps.

But Rickie insists, says, "Just five minutes. Really. I swear. Please."

We climb the steps of the condominium without any pretense of expectation.

Rickie's apartment is fragile and neat, furnished in a childish style that no one would imagine, given her physical and exuberant manner. In the tiny living room there are white lace curtains at the windows, two reproductions of Alpine landscapes on the walls, a lampshade of pink silk with blue flowers. Rickie points to a sofa and an easy chair; she says, "Sit down." She takes out a slide projector, places it on a chair; she removes one of the two landscapes to clear the wall opposite. She slips off her high heels, takes a few relieved steps, barefoot. Dru is seated on the floor, his back against the sofa; Elaine and I are behind him; Nesbitt is on the easy chair, his arms folded as if he were at a film festival. We stare at the white wall.

Rickie fits a cassette into the stereo, turns off the light, goes back to the projector in the darkness. Some strange piano music comes from the speakers, distilled, abstract, circular. Rickie lights a little marijuana pipe, inhales, doesn't offer it around. We look at the cone of light from the projector, and gradually the music echoes fragments of familiar tunes, purged and distanced in a shattered perspective.

Then Rickie begins to click the slides. They are details of objects and whole objects, but photographed as if their use or normal meaning were unknown. There is a bicycle propped against a tree, and it doesn't look at all like what it is. There is a straw chair; a gray stone; a box with a ribbon inside; the corner of a concrete wall; a little girl smiling, reproduced from an old Polaroid whose colors have altered.

"Me, age five," Rickie says. There is the edge of a bench, a hubcap of a car, a superhighway guardrail, gloves on a table. Every image is like the music we're hearing, alien and familiar at the same time, studied and casual. Rickie leaves each slide on only for a moment, and immediately clicks to the next, *click click click,* never stopping. We are all sitting there, staring, prisoners of her rhythm.

The loader ends; Rickie takes it away and fits another in; she resumes clicking at the same tempo. Elaine says, "Couldn't you go a little slower?" Rickie doesn't slow down in the least, kneeling in the dark area behind our backs. It isn't clear if she's doing this to keep within the five minutes she promised, or if she's not entirely satisfied with the slides, or if it's to get the effect she's getting; we can't tell if it's the marijuana smoke in the air that makes us transmit meanings to these images, or if it's the images themselves transmitting meanings to us.

There's a gray pyramid in a grassy clearing surrounded by jungle, and the slides end. Rickie turns off the projector, turns on the light again, turns off the stereo. She says, "There."

"What was it?" Dru says after at least half a minute, pointing to the wall, where she is already hanging the picture again.

"What?" she says, does a kind of pirouette.

Dru seems surprised at how elusive she is, how strange compared with when we came to pick her up, compared with ten minutes ago, in the car. I'm surprised, too; and Nesbitt is speechless. We remain motionless in our places. The music has left us with an odd vibration; or maybe we're only dazed, full of sleep.

Finally Nesbitt looks at his watch, looks at Dru; he says, "I don't know: shouldn't we be getting along?"

"Yes, yes," Dru says, relieved.

We say good night to Rickie, go down, careful at each step. Elaine says, "Isn't she wonderful?" In the street Dru looks up, and Rickie is there looking at us from a little balcony. She waves a hand, says, "Be well," in a tone slightly mystical and maternal and apprehensive and reassuring, and in the tone, also, of a superficial little girl.

Dru is seated at one of the two bars

Dru is seated at one of the two bars when I come down; he has already had breakfast, and it is clear that the agreeable vein of the past few days has been mined out completely. He taps his fingers on the little table, says, "I haven't wasted my time like this for *years*."

I order only a glass of milk, so as not to make him waste more; I drink it in four gulps. He looks at his watch, says, "What the hell's Jack doing?"

We return to the lobby, and Nesbitt is coming in at this very moment; he walks quickly toward us. He says, "You're on the eleven o'clock flight; we should get moving in about fifteen minutes." Again he is in control of his impulses, and doesn't show disappointment.

We go up to collect my suitcase, to witness the closing of Dru's. He throws in the final things without taking the slightest trouble to arrange them, presses the lid until he can make the locks click. A bellboy peers in at the open door; Dru points to the suitcase. But the bellboy has an envelope in his hand; he holds it out. Dru goes to the window to read it; his expression changes. Nesbitt and I look over his shoulder and read, without waiting for him to ask us.

The message is long this time, a whole page of penciled words in irregular shapes. It says: *Dear Friend, You are so dominated by the thought of controlling the things around you that you are not even aware of their meaning. You think you can place this, too, inside the boundaries you set for everything that comes into contact with your life. That is absurd. Your creative force is blocked and you cannot bring yourself to admit it, still less to admit the reason. Your work is a cold repetition of themes to which you gave intensity in the past, but now you use them like the ingredients in a recipe. The passion that drove you has been replaced by technical skill, sterile and irrelevant. You are divided among V. and J. and L., but your life has no equilibrium and neither does theirs. Now you can choose between following this line or allowing yourself to be caught up again in the urgency that leads to nothingness.*

Dru crumples the paper in his fingers; he says, "But who are they? How do they know about me?" He is pale with anger now. He opens the suitcase, takes out an envelope with the other messages he's received, scatters them on the bed. He says, "How dare they meddle in my life? And with that *tone,* as if they observed everything from some kind of higher vantagepoint!"

At the door there is another bellboy, for the suitcase. Dru motions him to carry it down; Dru takes all the messages and tears them up: in halves, in quarters, and again and again, until his hands are full of little scraps of paper. He says, "What do they think? Just because somebody's a director and generically unconventional and open to suggestions, do they think he'll be caught like a fool in the first trap that a gang of blackmailing idiot mafiosi set for him?" He throws the bits of paper into the wastebasket, sends the basket under the desk with a kick. He says, "Let's go to the airport. I've had a bellyful of this place."

We go down to the lobby. As we step out of the elevator, the voice over the PA is saying, "Mr. Resnik wanted on the telephone. Mr. Resnik . . . on the telephone, please."

Dru, still furious, goes to the desk, wrenches the receiver from the girl's hand. Nesbitt and I look at him, some feet away, as he presses the receiver to his ear, half closes his eyes, rests one elbow on the counter, repeats two or three times the same movements of the lips, hangs up, looks at the floor.

We move toward him. The bellboy with the luggage stands waiting nearby. "Who was it?" Nesbitt asks.

Dru doesn't answer; he looks away.

"What did they say?" Nesbitt asks, increasingly alarmed.

Dru shakes his head, says, "That tearing up the messages was a childish thing to do."

"And how the hell did they know you tore them up?" Nesbitt says. "How is it possible?"

Dru goes to a group of easy chairs; we follow him. Nobody sits down or knows what to do. Nesbitt says, "Was it the same voice as in La Jolla?"

"I think so," Dru says. He pinches the back of a chair.

"The same electronic tone?" Nesbitt insists.

"It isn't electronic," Dru says. "It's hard to describe. It's a strange, neutral sound, drawn out; as if each word could stand by itself, outside the sentence." He puts his hand on the back of his neck, says: "It takes such a damn effort just to understand what he's saying."

Nesbitt walks around him, says, "And he knew you had torn up the messages?"

"Yes," Dru says. "He asked me why I did it."

"Threatening?" Nesbitt says.

"No," Dru says. "There was a note of disappointment under the neutral tone. Or maybe I imagined that: I don't know." He slaps the chair a couple of times, kicks it.

Nesbitt looks at his watch, looks at the bellboy waiting on the other side of the lobby. He says, "We'll miss the plane. . . . "

"Forget the plane," Dru says. "Lend me a hand; I want to piece together those goddam messages."

I run to buy some transparent tape at the hotel's drugstore, I join them upstairs. The two of them are already at the coffee table, facing dozens of scraps of paper.

The task isn't simple, with the sentence lines rising and falling in ways hard to foresee. We try starting from the corners, from the hotel heading; we try various combinations of words, various juxtapositions of torn margins. First we reconstruct the message transcribed in printed letters, then those of one or two lines; we leave for last today's long message. This is odd, our rummaging like amateur archeologists among fragments of obscure yet peremptory judgments on Dru's artistic and private life. But Dru doesn't care, he just wants to put the messages together.

We try to follow the meaning of the sentences as we remember them; we proceed word by word. Nesbitt reads aloud as he cautiously puts the fragments together, says, " . . . you are divided . . . among V. and J. . . . "

101

" . . . and L.," Dru says, putting the crumpled scrap of paper after the others. He says, "There may be three people in the world who know about me and Jane. But nobody knows about Leena. Nobody. Not even my closest friends."

It takes us at least half an hour to piece together the last message. Then Dru smooths it out with the palm of his hand, folds it carefully and slips it with the others into an envelope; he stretches his arms and flexes them a couple of times, to loosen up.

Nesbitt goes to the window, draws aside the curtain. He says, "How the hell could they know you'd torn them up?" He slides the glass, steps out on the balcony to look at the windows of the other rooms overlooking the patio with the pool. I also look out, but there is no sign of spies with binoculars or long-range microphones.

Dru, his hands on his hips, throws his head back, turns it slowly to the right, to the left. He says, "The fact is, we're so accustomed to explain everything in rational terms, to look for a simple, mechanical cause behind whatever happens to us . . . "

"What do you mean by that?" Nesbitt says. He closes the window again. "What causes should there be, in this case? Transcendental? Paranormal?" His voice is worried, beneath his effort to sound sarcastic.

"Don't ask me," Dru says. He balances on one foot, holds the other.

Nesbitt goes to study the telephone closely; he unscrews the two ends of the receiver. He says, "Dru, any organization with a minimum of means is probably capable of collecting information about your private life and then using it to make an impression on you. . . . "

Dru bends, on one foot, until he is able to touch the ground with the fingertips of his free hand. He says, "But this isn't information anyone can collect."

Nesbitt looks inside the receiver, screws the pieces back in place again, says, "You know better than I do that the private life of a celebrity is never really secret; there's always somebody who knows something."

"I don't give a damn about my private life," Dru says. He almost loses his balance, puts the other foot down. He says, "What they say about my work is also true. It's *true*. And that's not something you can go and read in some article, since, according to what the reviews say, my pictures become more and more extraordinary and profound as I go on making them. And I can't think of a single reason why a gang of blackmailers would bother to come and tell me things like this, and, what's more, in such a complicated way."

Nesbitt looks at him, doesn't seem convinced, but he can't find anything to say in rebuttal. He goes and opens the closet, takes out Camado's stick; he examines it from one end to the other, tries to figure out if it contains some device, some mechanism.

Dru says, "The voice told me also that the secret is in green. He didn't explain what that meant. And he said that today we should eat only green vegetables and go near the water."

"*Green?*" Nesbitt says. He puts down the stick, sits on the bed. He says, "Anyway, if that means you're staying on a few more days . . . "

Dru says, "Yes, but let's get out of this room, if you don't mind." He makes for the door.

We go down, and as soon as we're outside the glass doors, a character dressed all in green comes toward us, stops in front of us, smiling.

Nesbitt seems uneasy, introduces him to Dru with an oblique wave, says, "Nick Hart, a director I'm discussing a project with."

Hart shakes Dru's hand for half a minute, says to him, "It's fantastic meeting you." He has quick eyes, semivertical hair; he speaks with an anxious shortness of breath. He says, "I've seen all your films at least ten times."

"Really?" Dru says; he continues staring at the green jacket of wide-wale corduroy, the green shirt and pants.

Nesbitt glides on, to lose him, says, "Nick, call me in a few days; we're leaving just now."

Hart begins to withdraw; he waves, but Dru says to him, "Why don't you come for a ride with us? We were thinking of going to the ocean."

So all four of us pile into the Mercedes; Nesbitt drives slowly; Hart and Dru are seated in the back, sizing each other up, waiting to see who'll make the first move. Finally Hart says, "It's amazing we should meet like this, because my movie that Jack's supposed to produce is practically a remake of *Two of Two,* which in my opinion is one of the greatest films of the last ten years; the idea is to take the exact same story but shift it to a science-fiction atmosphere and have all the parts played by *very* young actors, twelve years old at most, which if you ask me is a downright *challenge* in terms of language, apart from any consideration of the market, I mean: making something so complex and apparently so European into something simple and universal, into something that even a kid can identify with . . . "

I turn to look at him, the way he's adhering to Dru, who is probably wondering what the secret is in green, and I feel a stab of pain in my right leg; I cry out, Nesbitt brakes, makes the car rock, the tires squeal.

On the seat is a pin at least eight inches long, with a big

dark head. Nesbitt picks it up cautiously; he says, "What the hell . . ." I rub my leg; it's only a superficial prick, luckily. But the pin is sinister: sharp and rusty, the head bone or Bakelite, a dark brown rather than black. Dru has Nesbitt give it to him, looks at it closely without saying anything. The cars behind us blow their horns, swing past. Nesbitt starts up again, proceeds very slowly as far as Santa Monica, then takes a road along the ocean.

Dru, in the back, looks at Hart with a questioning expression; he holds out the pin to him, says, "What does it mean?"

Hart holds it in his hand as if he were afraid of being burned; he says, "It doesn't seem very friendly." He looks at Dru and me and Nesbitt, trying to figure out if we are making fun of him or testing him or what. He doesn't know where to put it down; he returns it to Nesbitt, who slips it into the glove compartment. Hart smiles in pure embarrassment, looks out, as if the landscape suddenly interests him.

We head north aimlessly for a while, then Dru says, "We don't have to go to San Francisco." Nesbitt turns at the first filling station, heads back.

At Santa Monica, Dru says, "Let's stop here by the water." Nesbitt pulls up beside a deck with some old people stretched out sunbathing; he stops outside a building set back a way from the traffic.

It's a fancy cafeteria, with a great variety of foods behind little sliding glass windows; silent customers pay and go outside to sit under the umbrellas. Hart fills his tray with roast turkey and quiche lorraine and potatoes and Russian salad and cheese and bread and yogurt and everything he sees. Dru takes only a bowl of pale lettuce; Nesbitt and I do the same. At the cashier's desk, Hart looks at our trays and is almost paralyzed with uneasiness.

We sit outside, on a terrace from which you can see the

ocean, beyond the palms along the road. We eat our lettuce leaves, not even seasoning them. Hart tries to compress his stuff on the tray to make it seem like less; he coughs. Finally he's so embarrassed he says to Dru, "I imagine they must have asked you this a million times, but where would you say your inspiration comes from?"

Dru has a breathy laugh, turns to look at the plate glass of the cafeteria. Hart pushes his quiche aside, hides it behind a cup of yogurt.

Dru says, "In this case? Or in general?"

Hart again makes an effort to understand the situation, but he fails; he says, "In general."

"I believe it's a cluster of suspended particles," Dru says. "You just have to activate a current and they come together."

"Then it's a process that can be controlled, once you know how," Hart says with a serious face. "It can be reproduced." He tries to open the yogurt without attracting attention.

Dru doesn't even look at him, says, "Not really. It's not that there are buttons ready and waiting, buttons that you can press at any time. It's a contact in the dark, mostly."

Hart nods his head, his nails scratching at the aluminum-foil lid.

"You can also quite easily activate a negative current, which assembles all the wrong elements," Dru says. "Or a closed circuit, with the same current moving in a circle. Or you can make the same connection ten times in a row without realizing it's the same. But the easiest thing of all is to stand there and grope in the dark like an idiot, hoping to get a shock."

Hart presses his thumb on the lid; he breaks the foil, and yogurt spurts all the way to his elbow.

———————

When we get back to the hotel, Elaine is sitting in an easy chair near the entrance; she stands as soon as she sees us. I almost have to make an effort to recognize her, dressed in white as she is now, her hair pulled back, her makeup lighter than last night. She seems much less nervous; she kisses all three of us on the cheek, says, "I just wanted to say hello to everybody; I'm leaving right away."

"No, stay with us," Dru says. The business of the voodoo pin hasn't put him in a good mood. He says, "If the rest of you will come upstairs with me for a moment, I'll just make a phone call, and then we can go see a film or something."

All four of us go up to his room. The moment we're inside, Elaine bends over and picks up an envelope from the floor. Dru and Nesbitt and I freeze; she doesn't seem to understand why we are so affected. Dru takes it from her at once, opens it, reads the message as he sits on the bed. He sighs, hands it to Nesbitt, who comes over to read it with me and Elaine.

It says: *Threats are only black magic and as such trivial. Your colors in order of age are green, yellow, and blue. Tomorrow you will be at Cancún and from there you will follow the signs. Keep the spiritual girl with you. You are protected.*

Nesbitt scratches his neck, says, "By threats they mean the pin, I suppose."

"I suppose," Dru says. He turns on the TV, turns it off.

Elaine looks at us as if she understands something, even if not everything; she doesn't ask any questions.

Dru mentions the other messages to her in a vague way; he takes them from the drawer of the night table and shows them to her. He says, "If you're the spiritual girl, I don't believe there should be any secrets."

She reads, nods her head yes, not all that surprised. Finally she says, "Yes. We have to follow the signs." She seems very calm and self-controlled, but a moment later she is moved, sniffs; she says, "Thanks," not to us, I think.

Dru looks at her, a few paces away; he goes and gives her a kiss on the temple; he says: "I'm glad you're here, too." His earlier puzzlement is now turning into euphoria; he slaps Nesbitt a couple of times, says, "You're *Yellow*, dammit, Jack!" He gives me a push, too; he says, "Do you realize what's happening to us?"

Nesbitt says, "I don't think so"; he looks at Elaine with worried eyes. He says, "And where is this Cancún place anyway?"

"In Mexico, the far north of Yucatán, I think," Elaine says. She has a ready air now, under her spiritual air: like a diver who is waiting to leap.

Nesbitt is driving to the airport

Nesbitt is driving to the airport in the midmorning traffic; he turns every few seconds to look at Elaine, sitting at his side. She's dressed in white, vaguely tropical style, with trousers tight at the calves and a little tunic with many pockets; she seems much less spiritual than yesterday evening. She pats her hair with one hand, says, "Miles will fire me when he finds out I've gone off like this."

"I'll call him," Dru says, looking out. "I'll explain that you're indispensable to me."

"I am?" Elaine says, even less spiritual than two seconds ago.

Dru points upward. We all crane our necks to see, and there's a dark hawk above the freeway; it's flying in our direction.

At the airport Nesbitt parks in a multilevel garage; still reluctant, pocketing the keys, he helps me with the four identical bags we bought in the hotel; he says, "There's time for us to change our minds."

"Oh, cut it out," Elaine says to him. She takes him by the arm, pulls him along, through a glassed-in passage that leads to an elevator down to the departure lounge. There, she says to him, "Dru and I are going to telephone; you and Dave handle the check-in." Leaning on the counter, Nesbitt turns to look at them, and I believe he realizes then how well they get on, seeing them together, side by side under the half-shell of pale blue plastic.

The lounge is a box on stilts connected to the airport and to the plane by two pleated tunnels. We sit on little chairs of molded plastic, each of us with a bag at his feet. Dru drums his fingers on the back of the chair. Elaine looks at the tips of her white shoes. We are tense: shaken and oppressed by the atmosphere. Nesbitt says, "Well, my secretary has the details of the flight and the hotel in Cancún and everything. If I don't phone her this evening to say we've arrived safely, she knows to inform the police."

Dru says, "My God, Jack," but he isn't amused, he chews his lips.

I try not to let myself get too involved in all these apprehensions; to keep myself out of them. There's a very old man, a sort of Mexican cowboy, seated facing me, leaning on a cane, tended by a much younger daughter or wife, who hands him a little box of mints at regular intervals. He takes one and with incredible slowness puts it in his mouth while he surveys his surroundings with a panning movement of his head. He's dressed almost like a caricature, with broad-brimmed hat and little boots with pointed toes and a belt with metal studs, a leather thong for a tie, silver-and-bead buckles; it isn't clear if all this is to impress somebody in Mexico or if it's his normal style. I concentrate on him for a while, until he seems so far behind the level on which everyone else moves that I have to stop and turn my head away.

The PA voice says we can board, the attendants remove the velvet rope blocking the tunnel, the passengers collect their bags.

In the plane, Dru observes with worried eyes the details of the aircraft, its condition: the scratches on the metal, the flaking signs, the patched paneling. He sits near an emergency door; I sit at the window opposite; Elaine and Nesbitt farther back. The other passengers are drab Mexicans on their way home for a visit or American couples or families on a holiday. Dru clutches the arms of his seat, looks out: the gray of the runway begins to flow beneath us.

Then we are high above the ocean, the old DC-10 creaking and tilting at the slightest turbulence. The aged Mexican cowboy is seated up front, his daughter or wife still handing him mints; there is a little blond boy crying and kicking in his mother's arms. A stewardess comes by with a drinks trolley. Dru writes in a notebook; he pauses to check the situation through the window; writes some more. I glance at a travel magazine with photographs of hotels and beaches and swimming pools and girls in bathing suits; I get up to walk a bit in the aisle.

Nesbitt and Elaine are seated, holding glasses of gin and tonic; they don't seem to be talking much. I say to him, "We still have a good two hours before landing."

"Ah," Nesbitt says. Elaine turns to look at a dozen noisy young men in the back rows: elaborately done hair, earrings and tattoos, black T-shirts with *Can't Cost* written on them.

They keep shifting their seats, throwing their legs over the arms, giggling and pretending to exchange karate blows, drinking beer. Some normal passengers look around, but without the courage to protest or to assume a really irritated expression.

Elaine gets up, says, "I'll be right back."

Nesbitt looks at her as she goes past the boys with the T-shirts, replies to some remarks of theirs, slips into a lavatory.

I sit in an empty seat behind his; we make generic conversation about the trip. He points to Dru seated up ahead, writing; he says, "I suppose all this business gave him an idea for another movie."

"Yes," I say, since he seems to be seeking confirmations.

He looks toward the tail of the plane; Elaine has already come out of the lavatory and is bent over to hear what the boys in T-shirts are saying. She seems to say no, then yes, accepts a can of beer, drinks a few sips. Nesbitt says, "There are some possible elements at this point. A director like him could make a murder story out of it, or a thriller, or a comedy. Or even a mystical story, if he wanted. He's such a genius." He turns again to look: Elaine, perched on a seat arm, is laughing, tilting her head. He says, "The question is, does he *want* to think of another film?"

"Of course," I say. The conversation is fairly uncomfortable, with us seated one behind the other like this.

Elaine comes back, slips into her seat. She says, "I was talking with those guys."

"They must have been interesting," Nesbitt says, filled with anger.

She says, "They're the Lonely Crowd. They're number four on the Top Ten this week."

"I don't think I've ever heard them," Nesbitt says, without looking at them.

"Yes, you have," Elaine says. She sings "Can't cost, no no, it can't cost . . ." inaccurately. She pats her hair, says, "They offered me a part in the video they're going to shoot now, but it's impossible to do two things at once." She says this in a tone of regret, which Nesbitt doesn't miss.

They sit still, ahead of me, for a few moments, without looking at each other. Then she gets up again and slips into the seat next to Dru. Dru shows her the little notebook he's writing in, explains something to her; she leans over to read with a demure expression.

We have a stopover at Monterrey, in a deserted airport. The very old cowboy gets off, along with all the other Mexicans; we remain waiting in the sticky heat of a small transit lounge, newly built. Elaine talks again with the musicians, introduces them to Dru. With him they are awkward, far more shy than anyone would have imagined. Joking, they ask him if he would direct their video; he says, "Why not?" One of them has a cane similar to Camado's, but with a series of holes so it can also serve as a flute. Dru asks him to play it; the musician holds it up, puts his fingers in the correct positions, but then shakes his head, says, "Some other time." The boys laugh. Nesbitt, sitting by himself, looks away. Outside, the sky is completely red.

Later, we've been flying for so long that we seem to vibrate, motionless in the dark, always at the same distance from three minuscule dots of light. But we are coming down; we are on the landing field of Cancún.

Outside, the air is even hotter and more humid than in Monterrey, real tropical air, thick to go through, as we walk toward the low buildings of the airport. Dru points to Elaine walking ahead of us with Nesbitt beside her; he says to me, "She's an incredibly sensitive girl, when she wants to be."

In the arrival lounge there are some kids touting hotels, insistent taxi drivers. Nesbitt goes and argues at the Hertz stand, where they can't find any trace of his reservation. The rock musicians very cordially say good-bye to Dru, pay a few more compliments to Elaine, who smiles until they're gone, and smiles a few seconds longer.

Finally a little boy from Hertz leads us outside, points to a white Ford, gives us the keys. Nesbitt asks him for directions to our hotel; the little boy gestures with his thin arms, recites information in distorted English.

We follow the road that curves away from the lights of the airport and proceeds in absolute darkness. There must be dense vegetation all around us; we see an occasional flash of it in the beams of the headlights. Nesbitt says, "Here there was nothing, until they had the idea of making it into a tourist center." He drives carefully, tests the car's controls. Then he looks in the mirror, says, "They're following us."

We look around, and indeed there are headlights behind us, maybe fifty yards away.

"They were waiting for us just outside the airport," Nesbitt says. "I saw them as they were pulling out. It's a Pontiac."

Dru says, "Accelerate a little." Nesbitt accelerates, but the headlights remain at the same distance.

There is no other light around, not the slightest sign of any habitation. In addition, we are dazed by the trip, by the vibration of the plane, the change in temperature and humidity. Nesbitt says, "We can't shake them, not with this car."

Dru says, "Thank God your secretary knows what to do, if we end up vanishing into thin air."

Nesbitt looks at him, looks in the mirror, more nervous than ever. But now there are lights; street lamps more and more frequent; houses and the concrete walls of a little artifi-

114

cial city, a car parked outside a bar. Nesbitt brakes, says, "I'll go in there and ask where the police station is."

"No," Dru says. "If they planned to do anything to us, they'd have done it by now. Let's go to the hotel."

Nesbitt stops all the same outside an ugly gray building, still unfinished. We wait for a few minutes in the light of the street lamps, but the other car is no longer to be seen. Elaine says, "Let's go, Jack"; Nesbitt drives off again.

The road leaves the little artificial city; it crosses another stretch of darkness thick with vegetation, and then it comes out into the open, running straight along the line of the sea. There is dim moonlight, then the light of a huge white parallelopiped, an American hotel, which suddenly looms up on our right. Nesbitt looks in the mirror again; the headlights have disappeared.

Now there are hotels on our left as well; we are on a spit of land with beaches and sea on either side. We go past cubes and pyramids and enormous spheres flooded by banks of spotlights; we read the neon signs until Nesbitt recognizes our hotel and slows down, turns into a drive as broad as a super-highway; he stops under a monumental marquee.

We check to see if the other car has followed us here, but nothing can be seen beyond the halo of light that enfolds the hotel. We climb the grand stairway that leads to the lobby.

Inside, Dru says, "Jeeezus." It's like being at the bottom of a gigantic well, made of balcony after concentric balcony onto which doors and doors and doors open for at least twenty-five stories; at the top the well is closed by a lid of veined glass. And we're not even at the bottom; the real bottom is six feet farther down, a kind of enclosed garden with flowers and trees and an artificial waterfall, garden chairs, a grand piano. Two of the trees are dead: dry and whitish like vegetal ghosts.

The clerks behind the reception desk look at us with suspicious eyes; they ask for our identification, hand us forms to fill out. They hesitate over their ledgers and their telexed reservations, they tap apparently at random the keys of a computer, ask us other questions, inquire how long we want to stay. Nesbitt says we don't know; they become even more distrustful. Dru says to Elaine, "It's like setting a couple of cops to pilot a spaceship."

A sumptuous spaceship, too, made of imported materials, marble, gilt, dehumidified and ventilated, every corner polished. Two American couples in shorts and flowered shirts pass us, heading for the elevators, their tanned faces filled with sleep.

Nesbitt manages to resolve the bureaucratic complications, makes them give us our keys. He stumbles, to be close to Elaine, looks nervously at the glass entrance. A valet takes us up to the ring where our rooms are, leads us along the circular balcony. Dru leans over and looks down, aghast; he says, "There should be a court of law for things like this." Elaine slips into the first room; Nesbitt, in order to follow her, immediately gives too big a tip to the valet, who stares at him with surprise. Dru takes the next room, and I have the last of the three.

The rooms are enormous, with a vestibule and a dressing room adjoining the bath, marble shelves, king-size bed, a Frigobar full of whiskey and gin and soft drinks, a twenty-eight-inch TV, a panel of buttons for air-conditioning and music and the curtains. On the coffee table there is a basket of exotic fruit wrapped in cellophane; a little slip of paper explains that the fruit has been disinfected and is perfectly edible. I eat half a papaya, sitting on the bed, thinking what a crime it is to be in a place like this so completely alone. I shower for at least fifteen minutes under the atomized spray; I use two or three snow-white towels, drop them on the floor; I dress and go downstairs.

Nesbitt is at the bottom of the great well, near the grand piano. I go and sit down beside him; we look up. Nobody can be seen, they must all be in bed already, even though it's only eleven. We listen to the sound of the waterfall, the hum of these millions of watts of light. Nesbitt says, "It would be nice to know at least how long we have to stay here."

Dru and Elaine come from one of the elevators together; they walk toward us. Dru says, "Let's see if we can find something to eat."

But the only thing open is a bar on the first ring, and a waitress tells us it's about to close. Dru asks me to explain to her in Spanish that we're dying of thirst; she says in English that all she can give us is fruit frappé. We drink it with long straws, sitting at a little crystal table; the drinks are sweetish and artificial. Then we follow some arrows that say SWIMMING POOL; we leave through an automatic glass door.

Outside, the air is again hot and humid, but it's pleasant at this time of night. We follow a pebbled path to a big pool in the form of a lake, with a cocktail hut in the center. On the other side of the pool a little orchestra is playing American favorites for a group of people dancing at the edge of the water. The ladies are almost all dressed in white; the men, in dinner jackets; they dance with a euphoria that seems almost staged. They must be rich Mexicans who are celebrating a marriage or some private anniversary; from here we can't make out the faces very clearly. It's a strange scene, resting precariously on the totally alien place. Dru seems struck by it, he remains motionless, looking on.

We climb a few steps that lead to a lawn with umbrellas

of coconut fiber and deck chairs, all illuminated by tiny spot-lights half-hidden in the grass. Four or five yards below, there is the sea; we can hear the regular breaking of the waves. We walk as if against the wind, even though the air is still.

We walk slowly, and Nesbitt touches my elbow, points to Dru farther back, a few paces from Elaine. Even at this distance and in the half-darkness it is obvious Dru has been gripped by some deep emotion, whether because of this place or because of the reasons for this journey. It's clear from the way he turns; from the way Elaine moves to his side and clings to him.

Nesbitt and I stay at the edge, in the attitude of intruders: hands in our pockets, sidelong glances. Nesbitt sits on a deck chair, lowers the back, stretches out; he crosses his arms behind his head. The sky is full of stars now, bigger and more luminous than usual. Dru and Elaine walk slowly on the lawn; they pause every few steps. Elaine makes some gesture; Dru shakes his head. We can't hear what they are saying; only the sea can be heard and the orchestra playing "New York, New York."

Sometimes

Sometimes, when I was six or seven years old, I would wake up in the middle of the night without any frame of reference, as if the one I had had the previous evening had been shattered into millions of anonymous particles, leaving me without the slightest idea of who I was, or what or where or when. It seemed to me I would never manage to regain my original perspective, I would have to choose one perspective among the many, all equidistant and all alien, which vibrated around me like luminous dust. Instead, I remained suspended in the intervening void, and then I turned back, dazed by faint echoes of unknown perceptions. I regained gradually the meaning of an object's form, its relation to the other objects in the room, the meaning of the room with regard to my being inside it. And as I did this, I realized how futile it was, like the work of a man shipwrecked in a strange land: to reassure himself, he starts giving familiar names to the elements of the landscape, building a conspiracy with himself that the first inhabitant of the place could jeopardize at any moment.

But I believed I had established enough footholds by now to obviate that danger, enough guide lights to provide the safety of immediate triangulation. It's unbelievable how a man can be convinced of the illusion of stability he has gradually constructed, until suddenly it dissolves and leaves him exposed, prey to an active and concentrated panic. Perhaps at the outset it's only an instinct for survival, an alarm set to go off when faced by the lack of identifiable outlines and rhythms and passages, but it soon extends to any condition that is mobile and impossible to control. It soon becomes a mania impelling us to universalize the most arbitrarily taken point of view, to deny that other views exist, to establish criteria, priorities, invent units and instruments for measuring everything visible, perceptible, and to proceed to give more and more names until not the slightest patch of shadow remains unclassifiable; it will be filed away under "patch of shadow," awaiting further progress. On a humbler scale, too, one tends to establish limits, to make one's thoughts spin like martens or wild rabbits always within the same perimeters, to strengthen year after year these perimeters until they become walls, which one finally considers natural boundaries. Everyone does it. Everyone breathes and moves in a confined area all his life, and if the walls he has around him don't let him see what is outside, when he is most curious, then he looks up and imagines above himself greater perimeters, even less easy to follow. But everyone remains curious, though he won't admit it; everyone hopes to find a crevice in the wall with a view that will surprise him. Everyone is attracted by the idea that there are other perspectives. Everyone is afraid of that.

Elaine is on the phone at seven-fifteen

Elaine is on the phone at seven-fifteen; she says, "You've got to come down at once, because the voice said we all have to bathe in the sea precisely at eight." She has such a definite tone that I don't think of questioning her. I jump out of bed, slip on my trunks.

The other three are seated at the bottom of the well, towels over their shoulders; they stand up the moment they see me. There is nobody else around yet, except for a couple of waiters along the lower balconies. We head for the exit to the pool. Dru looks as if he hadn't slept much, Elaine is at his side like an official interpreter, Nesbitt follows sleepily, dragging his feet.

Outside, the sun is still pale, the sky is only now beginning to take on some color. Near the pool, two musicians are dismantling the drum set, taking away the cymbals and the snare. We go up to the lawn with the coconut-fiber umbrellas, cross it, go down some little wooden steps to the beach.

We take off our shoes on the fine sand, contemplate the arc of white shore overlooked by other geometric monsters of hotels.

Nesbitt says, "Do you know why we have to take this swim?"

"No," Dru says.

"It's a purification," Elaine says in her vestal tone.

Dru kicks at the sand with the tip of his foot; he seems embarrassed by these subtitles.

"But did you ask the voice what they want from us?" Nesbitt says.

"If I understand correctly, they think that we want something from them," Dru says without looking at him.

Nesbitt has a puzzled expression; he bends over to collect a stick.

Dru says, "We have to have this dip in the sea and then go to Tis Talan, which is the negative center."

"Of what?" Nesbitt says.

"I don't know. Of the world, maybe," Dru says. "Or of this situation in particular. The voice said it wouldn't be easy: I didn't understand in what way. We have to burn the messages we've received, on a special stone chosen by Elaine, and we leave there all the negativity we have inside us."

Elaine looks to the sea with an inspired expression; she takes off her tunic. Underneath she has on a white one-piece suit.

"And then?" Nesbitt says.

"Then we have to come back to Cancún," Dru says. Obviously he is making an effort to recall the directions. He says,

"We have to leave this car and take another, an open car."

"A convertible?" Nesbitt says.

"Yes, or a jeep: I don't know. An open car," Dru says. "We have to take this car and stop and sleep in some extremely simple place and the next morning go to Atsantil, which is the contrary, the positive center. There we have to absorb as much as possible."

Elaine slips off her trousers and puts them next to her tunic. She says, "Eight minutes to go." She is even sexier than she seemed in her clothes: with an elegant back and a narrow waist, a well-shaped behind, ballerina's legs.

Dru and Nesbitt and I also take off our clothes. Dru has a suit bought at the Hilton, like mine; Nesbitt, a pair of flowered trunks, like a surfer's. He says, "But didn't he tell you who he is, or who they are?"

"I asked him what I should call him," Dru says, "and he said all you have to say is 'You.'"

Nesbitt shakes his head. It's strange to see the two of them together, in bathing suits: Dru with his light build made almost muscular thanks to laborious exercise; Nesbitt, neglecting his natural muscularity, already a bit overripe.

Elaine says, "One minute to go."

We all walk to the edge of the water, look at the gentle wave that breaks and retreats, leaving halos of dark gray that immediately evaporate to white. The sun is higher; it becomes stronger every second. Elaine looks at her watch, says, "Now." We all enter the sea at the same moment.

But it isn't clear if this is meant to be a kind of ritual immersion or, instead, if we can swim as we choose. Elaine walks into the water until it reaches her breasts; she stoops to wet her hair. Dru swims a couple of strokes and then stops, floats in place. I swim without moving too far out, turn, try to let the waves carry me. The water is transparent, perfect; you could stay in it all day. The only one really enjoying it is Nesbitt, swimming on his back without too much concern, splashing and making foam like a seagoing machine.

Dru and Elaine remain standing where you can touch bottom; they look out to sea, wet their heads two or three times. He keeps an eye on her, seems to entrust himself to her intuition at this moment. Then they both come out, say something to each other; he hands her a towel. Seen like this, they look even better together than yesterday at the airport, he dark and she fair between the pale blue of the sea and the white of the beach. They could be part of an ad for cigarettes, or maybe for whiskey.

I stay in a little longer, look at the bottom. It's ridiculous to be in a place like this in November and be made to get out after five minutes. I get out all the same, rather than spoil the effect of unity, even though no voice has said anything to me.

Dru, with a hand to his brow, looks at the enormous cylinder of the hotel behind us. Elaine rubs her hair, slightly bent forward, her legs apart, the suit clinging to her like a second skin. She notices I am looking at her; she smiles, quickly wraps herself in the towel.

Nesbitt wallows some more, then approaches the beach, lingering in the shallow water until Elaine says, "We have to go."

We go back to the hotel, the sun already beating down on our heads. Dru doesn't say anything; Elaine wiggles her hips beneath the towel. We go up to dress and collect our things.

When we meet again downstairs, the other hotel guests have begun circulating again: couples in various stages of tanning hurry along the balcony rings with beach bags and towels and shorts and plastic sandals and sunglasses. Dru says, "Let's get out of here."

We go to the front desk to turn in the keys. A man about thirty peers out among the clerks; he extends his hand to Dru, says he's the hotel manager, asks him to sign the guest book they keep for important guests. He has a persistent little smile, speaks with a good imitation of an American accent. He says, "Mr. Resnik, we would be highly honored if you would look at our presidential suite." He points to the veined glass lid at the top of the big well.

Dru tries, I believe, to figure out if this also has a meaning in the sequence of events; he says, "All right."

We go up to the top floor. The manager explains that he studied at the University of San Diego; that he's a great fan of European films. He talks like a politician about how he wants the hotel to be a second home for those who use it; about how he and his staff make every effort to establish a truly friendly relationship with the guests, without servility but also without impersonality. As he leads us along the top ring, he says, "We have guests who live here for six months of the year," as if he were speaking of a commune instead of a place that costs four hundred dollars a night. A bellboy slips ahead of us, opens the door of the presidential suite.

The manager rapidly points to the curtains; the bellboy, like a shadow, goes and presses a button to open them, reveals the spectacular view over the sea. The manager says, "President Reagan stayed here, and also our own president; but, of course, private citizens also can stay here." We look down: the long white beach, the sea where we were swimming a few minutes ago. He says, "You see the barracudas?"

"Barracudas?" Dru says, looking at those little dark shapes in the transparent blue.

"Yes," the manager says, smug about this, too. "We had to put up all those signs in case anybody got the idea of taking a swim in the ocean. In '85 the barracudas ate two workmen and an engineer from Cleveland, when the hotel was still under construction."

Dru runs one hand through his hair; Nesbitt says, "Holy cow."

We drive out of Cancún, head west. The road has recently been widened. There are flat stretches of reddish earth on either side, concrete platforms, worksites for new giant hotels or shopping centers or filling stations. The vegetation has been driven well back; there are dozens of bulldozers standing there, waiting to get back to work. Dru says, "They're doing a pretty good job of devastation, the bastards." Nesbitt concentrates on the driving; Elaine, at his right, looks out, chews gum. The air-conditioning is on maximum; cold air blows inside.

Then the road narrows and the vegetation closes in again, thickens, interrupted only every now and then by an excavation or a pile of stones or logs. Elaine takes off her sandals, puts her bare feet on the dashboard. Dru looks at the trees flowing by. Nesbitt drives fast, by his standards, pushing the engine along the straight and empty road.

There is a red flag; a man in the middle of the road waves it frantically and signals us to stop. Nesbitt swerves to avoid hitting him, resumes speeding as soon as he has gone past. Dru and Elaine and I yell "Stop!" in overlapping voices; we fling ourselves forward to grab the wheel from him, to pull the key from the ignition. In maybe three seconds he brakes, the car stops, and there is an incredible BBBRANG! that rends the air; stones and clods fly in all directions; dust rises; pebbles clatter on the hood and the glass and the roof.

The dust settles slowly; the man with the red flag runs toward us, yelling and gesticulating.

Elaine looks hard at Nesbitt, her pupils dilated with fear; Dru looks at the reddish rent in the forest. Elaine says, "You almost got us all killed! How could you help but see him? He was in the middle of the road!"

"I *did* see him," Nesbitt says. He is pale now; his hands are shaking; he continues staring straight ahead.

The man with the red flag knocks on the window, shouting like a lunatic. He points to the effects of the explosion, points to the road, shouts the same words at least ten times in succession.

Dru rolls down the window, says, "We're sorry. Our friend didn't understand."

The man goes on yelling and making gestures, but with less and less energy. Other dust-covered men come out of some shelter, collect around the car. They point and comment; some laugh.

"Would you mind telling us what the hell got into you?" Elaine says to Nesbitt. She turns an indignant profile; she knows very well that the men outside are looking at her.

"I don't know," Nesbitt says. "I was looking at the road. I wasn't thinking about anything in particular."

Dru looks puzzled, says, "Maybe Dave had better drive."

Nesbitt gets out, goes around the car, says, *"Disculpa,"* to the workmen. The workmen look at him without much comprehension, go back to what they were doing along the sides of the road. I sit behind the wheel, drive off slowly. Seated in back, Nesbitt says, "I don't know what it was. I saw the guy with the flag, but he didn't *register*. Nothing like this ever happened to me before. It's absurd." At my right Elaine gnaws her thumb; she puts her feet back on the dashboard.

Now there is real jungle on either side, trees and trees, bushes and tall grass making two compact green walls. We proceed for miles without meeting anybody, then pass through a small village made of concrete cubes. There are children at the edge of the road, withered old women or old men dozing on the steps, dogs and dark piglets stretched out in the dust. From their immobility we can guess how hot it is outside.

We continue moving away from Cancún and pass through another couple of villages, these made of huts of wood and boughs instead of concrete, round instead of square, less symmetrical with the road; there are little vegetable gardens, narrow paths that go off into the vegetation. Dru says, "Sooner or later they'll manage to ruin everything even here."

Elaine turns on the radio, twists the dial, stops at an ugly Mexican song, rasped and mauled by static. Dru says, "Turn it off, for God's sake." She turns it off; she looks out, with the expression of a little girl on a holiday with boring parents. It's incredible how little she cares about maintaining any coherence of character; even with respect only to last night, or this morning.

The car is sluggish, unresponsive. Cold air blows into my face; it's giving me an ache in one temple. There is no variation in the landscape, no variation of route.

I look at the road, pensive, and suddenly Elaine and Dru and Nesbitt are pressing at me from all sides, yelling like crazy, "Dave!" There is no obstacle, nothing unexpected in the middle of the road, but all the same I jam on the brakes, try not to swerve. Elaine opens the door the moment we stop, throws herself out; Dru and Nesbitt also jump out on either side. I get out, too, and all three of them look at me as if I were a monster. I don't understand; I say, "Are you all out of your minds?"

"You were doing *a hundred*," Nesbitt says.

"And you wouldn't answer," Dru says; he is watching me closely.

I say, "But I braked the moment you told me to. I was driving all right, and you all jumped on me."

"You had this blank stare," Elaine says. "You looked hypnotized or something."

And there's no way of knowing if it's true or if they are completely under the spell of the situation; we'd need a video camera to find out. We look at one another sideways, near the white car in the full sunlight; we look at the deserted road. The heat is terrible; there is a steady buzz of insects from the vegetation all around. My brow is soaked with sweat, my shirt is sticking to my back.

With one hand on her hip, Elaine says, "Maybe it's a sign that we shouldn't go to the negative place."

Dru pulls a leaf from a branch, crumples it. He says, "They warned it would be difficult."

"But maybe they've realized it's too dangerous," Elaine says. "Maybe they're trying to stop us."

Nesbitt looks up at the sky, points a finger. There is a hawk flying north, more or less like the one we saw in Los Angeles before leaving. We watch it until it's far away. Elaine says, "I'm thirsty."

Dru sits at the wheel; we drive off slowly; the conditioned air freezes our sweat on us.

We proceed in silence for at least half an hour before coming to a village. Dru pulls up at a Coca-Cola sign; we get out.

There is an old Indian sitting on a straw chair on the other side of the road; five or six children come out from a path; a fat woman is in front of the store. We move slowly, close the doors awkwardly. We feel as if we had been traveling for weeks.

The store has a packed-earth floor, a damp, stifled smell. There are old cans and cardboard boxes on dark wood shelves; rusty hooks hang from a beam, strings; little jars of nails and corks stand on a ledge. There is a jar full of candies next to the scales; sacks of sugar in the semidarkness. The fat woman goes around behind the counter and looks at us, waiting. The children come inside and stand near the door, staring at us, some balancing on one leg. We are paralyzed, we sniff the air without moving.

Finally Elaine signals to the fat woman; she says, "Coca-Cola, please." She pronounces the words distinctly, as if she were acting in a film set in black Africa in the thirties, in her white semicolonial outfit.

The woman goes and opens an old refrigerator, takes out four bottles. On the shelves inside there is also a piece of butter, a little melon, an open carton of chocolate milk.

We drink silently, in long sips; tears come to our eyes. We look at the meager merchandise on display; the children continue staring at us. Dru puts the empty bottle down on the counter, points at the jar of candies, signals the woman to give him some. She takes out a little handful, drops them on a piece of brown paper. Dru says, "More," signals more. She spills another handful, reluctantly. She folds the paper into a little packet, weighs it on the old scales of black cast iron.

Dru goes and gives the candies to the children. The children don't move. They have nothing childish about them, except for the lightness of their movements because they are small. Dru turns toward the fat woman, points to the children, the candies. He says, "They're for them." The woman translates rapidly; the children come to take the candy. They have a distant manner; they don't say thanks, nor do they seem particularly happy. They go out on the path.

Nesbitt pays; we go back outside in the sun. Elaine crosses the street, goes and washes her face at a trough. She also wets her feet and forearms, sprinkles her head. The old Indian on the chair signals her to turn off the faucet; he repeats the same gesture two or three times. Dru takes off his shirt, puts it back on again. Maybe it's only that we're impressionable, or else we're being hit directly by the negative radiations.

We proceed further, and there is no sign of Tis Talan in any direction. Nesbitt says, "It's very odd." By now we tend to see anything as an oddity or a coincidence of some kind. The road makes a curve, then runs straight again through the vegetation.

Dru turns off the air-conditioning, rolls down the window, allows a wave of hot air to enter. We drive at forty miles per hour, sweating, legs nervous, we're fed up with the trip. Every now and then we look up but see only crows. Then there's a sign on the other side of the road; it says TIS TALAN. Dru turns, takes a dirt road.

We pass a thicket of trees, and suddenly we're in a big dusty lot cluttered with buses and cars, people going in and out of a kind of shed-café, souvenir vendors, families with children and cameras and Thermos bottles. It's incredible, after all these hours of driving without passing another car. Nesbitt says, "Obviously they all come from the north."

We leave the car, walk under the noon sun, through the exhaust fumes of the buses, whose motors are left running to keep the air conditioners in operation. We pass a gate in a fence, follow a path of packed earth. Dru stops; Elaine says, "My God." In front of us there is a clearing the size of ten baseball diamonds put together; in the clearing there are enormous gray pyramids. And, of course, it's significant that we've come here with the thought that this is the negative center of the world. The pyramids are indeed a violent presence, without the slightest connection with the low, gentle proportions of the landscape just beyond the clearing.

We walk, scattered, slowed down by the strength of the sun and the radiations of the pyramids. A few small forms climb up or down the first big steps, lean against the blocks of stone. In this heat most of the visitors must have taken refuge in the patches of shade or in the shed-café by the entrance, or in the air-conditioned buses.

We pass the largest pyramid. High steps lead to a kind of squat temple at the top. Nesbitt looks up; he says, "I read that they sacrificed fifteen thousand men up there, at one time. They slit their throats, one after the other."

Dru says, "The men didn't resist. They were convinced they would go straight to paradise."

"Think of the *blood* that flowed," Nesbitt says. I believe he's trying to impress Elaine, to act nonchalant in such an ominous setting. He says, "It must have been a whole *river* of blood."

Elaine says, "Cut it out, Jack," looks away. But the strange thing is that the story of human sacrifice seems nothing compared to the way these structures overwhelm the space and threaten anyone crossing it, with the brute strength of their weight and height and volume.

We go toward the center of the clearing. After a certain point there is no one but us; the tourists don't dare venture out into the open like this. We are oppressed by the heat and dazzled by the light, stunned; all four of us drag our feet. When we are at the farthest pyramids, we turn to look back, and from this vantagepoint the scene is almost unbearable. Dru takes from his pocket the envelope with the reconstructed messages; he says to Elaine, "Have you any idea where to burn them?"

Elaine tries to put on an inspired face, but the sun is too strong. She says, "I have to think about it."

We move around the last pyramid. There is still a brief stretch of short grass; then the jungle resumes. Among the leaves we see other blocks of gray stone, fragments of edifices covered by earth and vegetation, as this whole place once was. Elaine looks around, sighs.

Nesbitt sits in the shade of a tree, wipes his brow with his sleeve. Dru looks at the slanting wall opposite us, gray and final. Elaine says, "I'll walk around a bit to see if I can find the stone." She goes off slowly, her hands in her pockets; she disappears behind the pyramid.

I walk, skirting the jungle. There are steps, parts of enclosures or destroyed buildings, even a little tunnel that once led from somewhere to somewhere else. It's probable that the available funds were all spent to excavate the pyramids and nothing was left for this less monumental part.

I also go toward the shade, but it is a damp, heavy shade, offering no relief. Dru shifts some pebbles with the tip of his foot. Nesbitt is holding his head in his hands; he breathes slowly. We wait.

Finally Dru says, "Where the hell has she gone?"

Nesbitt stands up, goes toward the far pyramid, which closes off our view of the clearing. He says, "I'll go look for her," and also disappears behind the gray wall.

Dru is dying of the heat but he won't come out of the sun. He says, "Maybe she's out there checking each stone, one by one, like some kind of diviner."

There is a snapping sound; we turn, but nobody can be seen. Maybe it's some animal or forest bird, or a limb has broken of its own weight. Dru hesitates; he also comes and sits down under the leaves.

We wait another quarter of an hour, then the idea of staying here idle becomes so exasperating that I stand up; I say, "I'll see what's going on."

Dru says, "Try not to vanish like them."

I pass between the western side of the pyramid and the lowest wall, come out into the clearing. Now it really does look like an immense baseball diamond where menacing spacecraft have landed, the grandstands have disappeared, the fans have run off except for a few stragglers who wander around, dazed by the shock, unable to take in what's happened.

I wander at random, my brain cooked and my legs heavy, without the slightest energy for searching. In the distance, toward the front gate, there is a little white form struggling down the big steps of a pyramid; I wave to her, but at two hundred paces she turns out to be much clumsier and heavier than Elaine; with a husband not far off, taking her photograph.

I hear a shout, "Elaaaaaaine!" The shout travels well through the space; three or four human ants turn, in the most visited part of the clearing. I head for the source of the sound, see Nesbitt at the top of a pyramid, his hands on either side of his mouth. I shout "Hey!" to him. He looks down, seems disappointed at seeing me. He shouts again a couple of times in different directions, then climbs down. He is filled with anguish, soaked with sweat. He says, "She's not here. I've looked everywhere."

I say to him, "Maybe she's already with Dru." We go back to the end of the clearing. Nesbitt stops continually to look over his shoulder; he turns around, walks backward. It's like swimming in the midst of a fleet of warships.

Behind the last pyramid, Dru is more or less where we left him, crouching before a little fire on a stone.

"She hasn't come back?" Nesbitt says.

"No," Dru says, not raising his head. There is a streak of blood on his forehead, from a little cut. He pokes the fire with a stick, stirs the pages to make them burn better.

Nesbitt looks at the cut on his forehead, says, "What happened to you?"

Dru points to a branch above him, says, "I struck it as I was looking around for the right place, so maybe this is it." He continues to concentrate on the fire until the messages are only a little pile of dull black scraps, which crumble as soon as he blows on them.

Then we are all three staring at the ashes on the stone, and a man comes out of the tunnel to our left. I don't actually see him emerge, I see him already at the mouth of the tunnel. He is short, with a cap of shiny hair, an aquiline nose, and very black eyes. He looks at us with faint irony, looks at the remains of the fire. He says, "Is everything all right?"

It's a bit like when we saw the two men in the corridor of the hotel in Los Angeles: there is again a time shift, and when we realize that the character is not a guard or a guide or a souvenir vendor, he has already gone back into the tunnel, disappeared.

We run after him; Dru is the first to enter, Nesbitt and I follow. The tunnel is not as low as it seemed; we can walk erect without our heads touching. We pass through it rapidly in single file, by light that comes from the aperture perhaps a dozen yards ahead. The ancient stones are covered with mold, mineral salts; the earth beneath our feet is compact, resonant. We come out at the other end, and there is nothing but tall grass and thick woods.

Nesbitt bends to look, says: "He must at least have left

some footprints." But there isn't the slightest trace of any trampling. Nesbitt takes a few steps, to see if the grass flattens beneath his feet; it does. He says, "How the hell . . . " We prick up our ears; from the brush come only insect sounds and the cry of birds. Dru leans back against the stones of the tunnel.

We pass through it again, come out behind the pyramid. We look at the stone on which Dru burned the messages, and there is no trace of ash, no scorching from fire. Dru looks at me and Nesbitt with a kind of childish amusement in his eyes. He seems much more cheerful than when we arrived; younger, even. He says to Nesbitt, "Do I seem different to you?"

Nesbitt takes half a step backward to study him better. He tilts his head, says, "Maybe a little bit shorter."

Dru says to me, "What do you think?"

"I don't know," I say; even though he does seem to have lost perhaps half an inch.

Dru laughs, says, "I don't know what it is. I *feel* shorter. Not much, just a little."

Nesbitt goes over to him, measures himself, his shoulder against Dru's. But the ground is too uneven to make anything clear, and for that matter nobody remembers exactly what the difference was in their height before. In the end we give up. It is a moment in which you could believe anything, without any limit.

We cut diagonally across the great clearing. The sun is still beating down hard, but we walk with less difficulty. The presence of the pyramids no longer seems to involve us so much; their radiation has retreated into the background. Only Nesbitt is still tense, again in anguish because of Elaine; he looks in all directions. Every now and then he breaks away from us and reconnoiters at a little trot, checking around the corner of a pyramid. He returns short of breath, says, "Nothing." He looks at Dru for some kind of counsel or reassurance. Dru says, "Maybe she's waiting for us at the car."

In the part of the clearing near the entrance there are now more people than when we arrived: couples, families, whole groups milling around and taking photographs. We go back to the dirt lot, among the parked buses and cars, but Elaine is nowhere to be seen. Nesbitt goes all the way to the paved road; he comes back, shakes his head.

We go into the shed-café next to the gate. There are tourists swigging Coca-Cola and waiting at the door of the rest room, wiping handkerchiefs over their foreheads, moving among the fabrics and fake handicrafts. Here, too, Nesbitt checks everywhere; he looks out the little windows. Dru asks for mineral water, but there isn't any; he says, "We can't go on drinking junk," has the man give him a clump of bananas. Nesbitt pays; for all his distress, he manages to calculate that for only ten dollars we could fill the car with bananas. We leave through a door in the back, sit on three straw stools in the shade of an old fig tree. There is also a table; this must be the place where the man running the shed eats. The fence enclosing this part of the clearing is a few yards away, hidden by trees and bushes.

We eat the bananas, one after the other; scented and sweet though they are, they do little to quench thirst. Nesbitt stands, sits down again, stands again. He says, "I'm going to look for her some more." He goes off quickly, his shirt soaked with sweat.

Dru and I remain seated in the shade. Dru stretches his legs, sways back on the stool, looks at the leaves above us. The presence of the pyramids is screened by the vegetation; the presence of the parking lot, by the shed behind us; we are in a kind of neutral zone.

Dru says, "Last night I asked the voice why they chose me particularly for this contact. The voice said for what I was, not for what I did. Which may be poetic, but it's not clear."

The door behind us opens; the man looks at our stools with possessive eyes, but Dru turns, so irritated that the man withdraws at once, closes the door again.

Dru says, "What are they expecting of me? Am I supposed to make a propaganda film for them? A kind of giant commercial to convince people that there is something beyond us and we have to stop ruining this life and ruining this world?"

I don't know what to say to him; I finish the last banana.

He says, "What's sure is that they know a great deal about what we do and think, and they've set up this whole chain of places and atmospheres apparently full of meanings. But you can't help wondering: If they have this incredibly panoramic view of things, if they don't have to take time and space into account or the physical laws that hamper us every time we try to turn our fantasies into something real, why, then, do they have to send anonymous messages written in such a crude hand? Why do they have to use the phone to talk to us? Shouldn't they be able to do it anywhere, at any moment?"

We are immobile in the thick air, and there's a snap, a hoarse voice says, "Are you there?"

We wheel around; Nesbitt arrives, running around the shed, even more anxious and sweaty than before. He says, "She's nowhere to be found. I can't understand what's happened to her."

We follow him, go out into the dusty lot filled with noise. We move a few steps among the cars, parked or pulling away, and we see Elaine get out of a little white bus. She jumps down and immediately turns, as if she were coming instead from the clearing and the pyramids, so that in the confusion of movements and moods, when she joins us, it's not clear whether she had some connection with the bus or not. She smiles, says, "Sorry. I saw hundreds of stones, but not the right one, I'm afraid."

"We found it on our own," Dru says.

Nesbitt is two paces from her, and his anxiety turns into rage in the space of two seconds. He points to the white bus that now is slowly crossing the parking lot; he says, "What the hell were you doing in there?"

"Where?" Elaine says.

Nesbitt runs, chases the bus, overtakes it, bangs his hand a couple of times on its side, on the rear window. The bus accelerates; Nesbitt tries to keep up with it, runs like a madman, but he can't do it; he gives up, stops and watches it go off, coughing because of the dust. He comes back to us, to Elaine, shouts at her, "What the fuck were you doing with those bastards while we were worried sick about you, like the fools we are?" He grabs her arm, shakes her.

She steps back, says, "Have you gone crazy? What are you talking about?"

"You know very well," Nesbitt cries, not letting go. "Cheap whore!"

Dru restrains him, says, "Calm down, Jack."

But Nesbitt doesn't hear him; he yells, "You can't act like that! Not giving a lousy damn about anything, even in a situation like this!" Dru has a hard time preventing him from hurling himself forward again.

Elaine takes refuge behind me; she says, "All I did was ask for a lift, so I wouldn't have to walk the whole way. . . . "

"The whole way from where?" Nesbitt cries, almost without any voice left. "And you were to be the spiritual girl, with all those lousy inspired airs!"

A family of tourists, bloated and pale, watches the scene, leaning against their car; two kids, souvenir vendors, giggle and point. An enormous bus is swinging around a few yards away, stirring up clouds of dust, covering Nesbitt's voice with its noise.

Dru pushes all of us toward the car, says, "We knew this was the negative place. Let's get out of here fast."

The car is an oven; the air conditioner takes at least five minutes to cool it off. I drive, check the speed every few seconds, before the others can.

From time to time at the side of the road there's a row of two or three Indian kids carrying bundles of twigs or single logs on their backs. They walk half-bent, their little dark faces grave, as if they could go on and on for whole days. We pass them quickly, go a good twenty miles before we arrive at a village.

The light has been gone for at least an hour

The light has been gone for at least an hour when we arrive at Cancún and leave the car in the Hertz parking lot. In a prefabricated trap of an office, Nesbitt negotiates for a jeep, Dru and I and Elaine wait beneath the neon lamps. It isn't at all clear that we've left our negative tensions at Tis Talan; we're nervous and tired, irritable with one another. Elaine paces back and forth, hums a repetitious tune, offers some chewing gum to Dru, who says, "No."

An attendant brings us an old red jeep; Nesbitt climbs behind the wheel before Dru can issue other instructions. Elaine slips into the back with me, so as not to be close to Nesbitt. We go away from the lights, toward the south.

It's different crossing the night like this, without filters or shields, with the air coming at us full of the sweetish scents of the forest and calls and rapid trills and cracking sounds, rustling boughs. The dim headlights reveal the road only a few yards in advance; the engine runs slowly, roughly. The sensations from our surroundings are so strong, it's hard to remain concentrated on our individual resentments; we allow ourselves to relax gradually as we proceed. Dru says, "Now *anything* can happen. We no longer have any weapons against chance."

"That's true!" Elaine shouts, against the wind. "We're travelers in space!" She has one hand on her hair, but it flies all around nevertheless; it strikes my face, whichever way I bend. Her hair is perfumed, soft. Only Nesbitt seems not to participate in the atmosphere, gripping the wheel as he does, tensed to watch the road.

We slice through the darkness, sniff the air, and listen to the sounds, excited by the idea of going off like this, blindly, leaving behind the few points of reference we had. The tourists are all up north, sealed in hotels built in the form of cubes or wells or pyramids; the cars and buses are motionless in the parking lots; we are the only travelers stirring tonight.

Then, in the beams of the headlights, we see two Indians standing at the edge of the road. They are staring at the other side, too far apart to be able to speak to each other, immobile and waiting, incredibly lost in nothingness. Dru turns to look, but they are already gone; we might even have imagined them.

Nesbitt drives for another hour, maybe more; he goes on and on. For two days we've been on the move almost without eating, but I don't seem to be particularly tired or hungry. Elaine fiddles with her bag, takes out a sweater; she clings to the back with one hand, loses her balance, and falls against me, straightens up almost immediately. I don't do much to keep my distance; I am close to her, it's as if the seat were four inches narrower.

Nesbitt says to Dru, "Didn't he tell you where we should stop?"

"All he said was, a very simple place," Dru says.

"Here there doesn't seem to be anything," Nesbitt says. "Simple or not simple."

And almost immediately there is a white sign on our left, YUKO LINDO CABINS ON THE SEA RESTAURANT. Nesbitt brakes, turns onto a narrow dirt road.

For ten minutes Nesbitt drives as if afraid of entering a trap at any moment. There are crickets all around; a colder and damper gust of air, perhaps from a canebrake. Then we are at the end of the little road; we stop outside two white buildings connected by an arch. We jump down, stiff and dazed by the wind. There is only one window alight, half open. Beyond the arch, palms can be seen, in the dim moonlight that surfaces little by little from the darkness.

We go through a door on which RECEPTION is written, into a white room with a beamed ceiling. It's likely this originally was a mission. Nesbitt hits a bell on the desk two or three times; nobody appears. Elaine has a puzzled expression; she puffs out her cheeks. Dru looks at some cloth hanging on a wall, narrow horizontal stripes of intense colors. I have no wish to go back outside and drive on the dark road.

Nesbitt rings the bell again; a young man comes through a doorway. He says, "Please excuse me," finishes buttoning his shirt. Nesbitt asks him if there are three cabins available. The young man says, "All you want," smiles, makes us pay in advance. He says, "If you want to eat, we have a restaurant on the sea; it's open all night."

Outside, Elaine insists on driving to the cabins. She does this in her spiritual-girl air, as if it were a symbolic act. She drives with the headlights off, barely misses a couple of palm trees. We are in a genuine palm grove; dark, close trunks, leaves that shut out the sky. Elaine drives jerkily, in first gear, makes the engine cough. Nesbitt and I are clinging to the seat, but Dru once more seems filled with admiration; he says to her, "You should have driven the whole way."

Elaine stops with the hood in a bush. The cabins are wooden huts arranged in threes, in the shape of a U. By pure chance we are actually in front of our three; Elaine says, "You see?" From the other huts, almost in the palm grove, no lights or sounds come; there are no outside lights. Dru says, "I don't think it would be easy to find a place much simpler than this."

Inside, too, the difference is incredible between here and where we were last night. There are two plain beds, two straw chairs, a naked bulb, an old ceiling fan, blinds with rough slats at the windows. The bath is tiny; a trickle of yellowish water comes from the faucet; a handwritten note says *Do not drink*. There is a filled water jug on a shelf; it smells of disinfectant.

I go back outside, wait with Dru and Nesbitt until Elaine also comes out. She has put on a blouse, white slacks, has retouched her eye makeup, combed her hair. She takes a couple of exuberant steps, says, "Let's go eat something now!"

We walk among the palms and the bushes and the empty cabins, in search of the restaurant; it takes us ten minutes to find it. Nesbitt says, "How can they afford to keep it open, if it's always like this?"

The restaurant is a wooden shed longer and wider than the other buildings, with a roof of coconut fiber and decorative beams over the entrance. Inside, a waiter and a cook are chatting next to a silent jukebox; they wave us a greeting. There is no one at the tables dimly lighted by yellow bulbs hanging from the ceiling.

We go and sit down at the rear. From the windows we can see the last of the palm trees before the beach, some glints of the moon on the ocean. In one corner there is a big cage with a sleeping toucan inside. The waiter comes and says that at this hour he can bring us only what he has. He goes back to the entrance and turns on the jukebox: a song shouted in a tremulous voice over a guitar base. Dru says, "Oh, Christ, no," signals to the waiter to lower the volume; the waiter turns it off altogether. Nesbitt and Elaine sit at an angle so there is not the slightest risk of their looking at each other.

The waiter comes with chilled beer and tacos, jars of sauces. He smiles, seems pleased to have customers even if it's so late. Dru fills a taco with red pepper sauce, eats one corner; he says "Baah." He's in one of his negative moods now, looking for an excuse to complain.

I say, "To me, they're delicious." One of the drawbacks of this job is that when you're not on a set with specific things to do, you don't feel like saying yes and agreeing with somebody all the time. I try to keep as far as possible from the conversations and the mental currents, reminding myself that I'm doing all this to learn a profession, but every now and then I get fed up, bored, with this role.

Dru looks at me as if I had just said his films make me vomit.

Elaine says, "Dave's right. They're fantastic." She gives me a look, what's more, instead of staring through me as usual.

The waiter brings more beer and four small lobsters; he says that's all there is. We must have been famished, because we clean the whole platter in a few minutes, without talking, hunched over our plates, and when we've finished, we relax, we sit more loosely in our seats. Nesbitt tells Dru about an egomaniac young director who made him lose a pile of money last year; Dru laughs.

I drink the second beer, too, it's so cold and pleasant, and it doesn't seem to be going to my head too much. The waiter collects the empty bottles, brings us full ones. Now only Elaine and I are drinking; Dru and Nesbitt ask for mineral water, exchange remarks on cinema. I tell Elaine about the movies I worked on as an assistant, about the low-budget miniseries I have in mind, and after a while we're talking as if we were having supper just the two of us, leaning toward each other. It isn't a situation that's created little by little; I realize it all at once. Dru and Nesbitt are at the right margin of my visual field, Nesbitt involved in telling about a script, Dru half listening. I try to tell Elaine something seductive about Europe; she listens, drinks, and looks at me.

The waiter comes back again, followed by a boy; the waiter says, "He'll make you banana flambé," in the circus tone of a ringmaster introducing an acrobat.

The boy opens a wooden tripod, lights a little alcohol burner, sets a big dark pan on it. Behind him a middle-aged woman appears, helping him by means of a series of glances.

I follow this scene intermittently; every time I look at the boy, he has advanced to the next stage, and the preparation of the flambé seems to go in jerks, like a film sequence from which frames have been snipped at random. Otherwise I continue talking with Elaine, bending toward her. And she bends toward me, leaning on one elbow, with the glass of beer in her hand. Dru and Nesbitt concentrate heavily on the flambé, as if they really were at a circus. Only, at a certain point Nesbitt turns to look at us; but he's embarrassed at having done it in such an explicit way; he snaps back to his earlier position, points a finger at the boy, asks him in pseudo-Spanish, "How old are you?"

The boy is shaking the pan over the fire with his left hand, stirring brandy and sugar in a bowl with his right; he looks up and for a moment loses his balance, like a tightrope walker endangered by the shout of a thoughtless spectator. The woman behind him winces, says, "Fifteen," without taking her eyes off his hands.

But I believe I'm beginning to feel some effect from all this beer, because my head is filled with disjointed impressions rather than real ideas. For example, it seems to me that Nesbitt continues assailing me and Elaine with a lateral wave of jealousy, and a moment later I am shielded by a kind of curtain that crosses the table diagonally; a moment after that, I am again in an intolerable position.

The boy is tense now. He signals; the woman behind him repeats the signal for the waiter near the entrance; the waiter turns off the lights; with a rapid move, the boy pours the brandy syrup into the pan and lights it, flaming the bananas. There is only the yellow-bluish light of the fire that flares up until it is licking the roof. We all applaud; the lights come back on; the boy bows. He watches for a second or two until the flames die down, then he shifts the bananas to our plates.

They are good, though not as good, of course, as the show. I don't know what flavor they would have to have in order to achieve that. I finish another beer, pour some for Elaine, who is drinking as much as I am. Then our heads are even closer, as we slowly exchange observations on our character traits, affirmations and denials, indirect but insistent compliments. Nesbitt now looks at us every few seconds, with an almost automatic movement of the head. I don't care about being discreet or diplomatic at this point, but I can't figure out how the situation will be resolved. We are all held by different tensions, insensitive and attached to our private attitudes.

Dru stands up, says to Nesbitt, "I have to talk to you about something." He points to the door at the other end of the long shed. Nesbitt hesitates, looks again at me and Elaine; he stands up reluctantly. Dru says, "Excuse us, we're going outside for a moment." I don't know why he's doing this, but it seems entirely natural to me, since it so completely corresponds to what I would like.

So Elaine and I are alone in the dim yellow light, with many bottles of beer on the table; with the palms and the tropical ocean in the darkness behind us. I am hardly aware anymore of what I say, but it's of no importance, because we are leaving words now, going into gazes, gestures, hints of gestures, premeditated gestures. Every now and then it occurs to me that Dru and Nesbitt could come back inside at any moment; I try not to look toward the door. I'd like to get up, but I can't muster the energy.

Finally I say to Elaine, "Let's get out of here," the way Dru might say it, and a second later we're outside on the beach, taking off our shoes, hopping on one foot to keep from falling.

The air is tepid, with no sound except the wash of the sea. I put an arm around Elaine's waist, under the smooth cotton of her blouse. We walk side by side close to the sea, but the situation isn't as involved as it could be; we have only this lateral contact.

I point to the dark wrinkled water, say, "Shall we?"

Elaine looks at me without answering. I give her a push, but she slips beyond my reach, so I take off my clothes and run into the water, make a surface dive. The water is warm, shallow; when I stand up again, it reaches only my knees. I shout to Elaine, "Come on!" She takes a few steps, hesitantly slips off her slacks.

I shout once more, "Come on in!" I sink into the water because there's a little breeze now. She comes toward me but doesn't want to dive in, doesn't take off her blouse. She smiles at me, keeps her distance so I can't splash her. I look at her pale legs, what little I can see of her white panties; I approach like a shark, try to grasp an ankle. She squeals, shouts "No!," laughs.

I swim a couple of strokes out to sea, but I'm reminded of the barracudas, and there are clumps of silken seaweed that brush against me; I immediately go back. I try again to pull Elaine in, grab her by the calf; she kicks, splashes water around. A second later, it begins to rain. It rains in big, fresh drops. They become thicker and faster in a moment, they spatter the water with little bubbles.

We go back to shore, laugh and stumble up the sandy slope, put our pants back on, soaked as they already are. We walk in a zigzag among the palms under this steady shower, and the temperature is absolutely perfect, our movements cost us no effort, there is no need to take shelter. I put my hand on Elaine's hip, and it occurs to me that of all the situations that have ever happened to me in my life, this is the closest to a film. It is all so vaguely real, easy, insubstantial, and predictable. Elaine and I stop; we look at each other very close, and a moment later we're kissing.

It's a watery kiss. There is water pouring over us, rainwater, without salt, and in some way it rinses the taste of Elaine's lips, her tongue. We stay in each other's arms for a long time, our shoes in one hand, the free hand pressed against the other's back. I have a mental image of Nesbitt looking for us, but it lasts no more than a fraction of a second. We separate, we walk, embracing, toward our cabins, as if that were the only thing in the world to do.

We arrive almost at once, without any space for thinking. No light filters through the blinds of the cabins of Dru and Nesbitt, no sign of life. We look at each other in the little patio formed by the three wooden huts; Elaine smiles. I clasp her by the arms, awaiting two or three alternative developments I've seen before somewhere. She pushes me toward the door of my cabin; she says, "Let's go to yours."

I hunt the key in my soaked pockets for God knows how long; I open the door. I can't stand up straight, I keep turning to Elaine. She bends over, sets her soaked shoes on the step before the door. It occurs to me that it might be better not to leave them quite so visible, but this thought, too, lasts only a moment; I set my shoes beside hers; we go inside.

I close the door and bolt it, and we are in the refuge of the cabin, under the immobile fan. I grasp Elaine by the waist, and we kiss again: like fish, almost, with liquid, silent tongues. I run my hands over her hips, over the blouse that is sticking to her skin. She has small breasts, a ballerina's breasts, with prominent nipples. She kisses my ear, my neck. I hold her tight and walk backward toward one of the beds. I kiss her forehead, nose, let myself fall back, pull her on top of me. She says "Hey!" The springs creak, giving way. It's more a cot than a bed, old and hard. We kiss and hold each other more strongly, we produce heat, I stroke her behind with a heavy hand; she is breathing harder. I roll her over on her side, move up to the buttons. There is knocking at the door. Elaine rolls away and is on her feet; she looks at me, alarmed, a couple of yards away.

More knocking: *bang bang bang* on the fragile wood. Nesbitt's voice says, "Dave! Dave!"

I also spring to my feet. Elaine whispers to me, "I'm going to take a shower." She slips into the bathroom, closes the door.

Nesbitt is hammering on the door; he yells, "Dave! Open up!"

I go to the door without making any noise; in a pause between knocks I put an eye to the peephole: Nesbitt facing me, looking aside, facing me. He moves his head in jerks, like a caged animal, with exasperated eyes. He knocks again, shouts, "I know the two of you are in there!"

The door moves under his blows; if he started kicking it or hit it with his shoulder, he would surely knock it down.

As soon as he stops, I look again, see him turn, go furiously around the cabin. I slip along the wall, keeping my head down; I close the blinds an instant before he arrives to look through them. He sees the slats closing, however; he comes back and bangs on the door, shouts, "Open up!" in a voice that has gone entirely to pieces.

Now I really don't know what to do, because staying shut up in here doesn't seem the behavior of a gentleman; on the other hand, Elaine and I have said hardly a thing to each other so far; we don't have much of a basis for mature discussion. I go and knock on the bathroom door. Elaine says, "Come in"; she unfastens the bolt for me.

She really is taking a shower; she moves, a hazy pink, behind the plastic curtain. I say to her, "What are we going to do?"

She turns off the water, reaches out for a towel, wraps it around herself. She says, "I'll explain everything to him. I'll tell him we weren't doing anything wrong." She slips past me into the room, without smiling at me or anything.

I look again through the peephole: there's nobody in sight.

151

I try to figure out if Nesbitt is in ambush beyond the range of the little circle of glass, but it seems not. Elaine has already put her wet clothes back on; she rubs her hair with a little towel. She looks at me without expression, perhaps thinking of something to say to Nesbitt. I open the door: outside, it's stopped raining. Elaine says, "I'll be going."

I step aside to let her go out; I say, "Are you sure?" My head is incredibly confused, with overlapping images of three or four possible reactions. I see myself detached, allowing her to leave; dragging her back inside; going out and facing Nesbitt. None of these possibilities is a complete sequence.

She looks at Nesbitt's lighted window, says, "Don't worry. I'll tell him the truth: that I was just taking a shower." She stands on tiptoe, gives me a conclusive kiss, a surface kiss. She collects her shoes from the stoop, quickly goes off.

I close the door again, and I suddenly feel alone and abandoned as never before in my life. A moment ago I was sure I had some cause for smugness, seeing her leave like that. But now there are only traces of her in this room: the prints of her wet feet on the floor, the rumpled cover on the bed, the towel she used to dry her hair. It seems to me impossible that I let her go back to Nesbitt; apparently I'm allowing myself to be swept into a current of predictability, not even digging in my feet. I turn on the ceiling fan, watch the blades spin; I turn it off.

I slip on my pants, go out to look at Nesbitt's cabin. All the water that came down is already evaporating; it saturates the air with minuscule droplets. Elaine's high voice can be heard, the constricted voice of Nesbitt; noises perhaps of chairs or beds being shifted. I go back, walk in circles with my heart hurting me. Somebody knocks at my door.

Outside, there's Elaine, with her bag in her hand and a

furious face. She comes in, says, "He *slapped* me!" She flings the bag in one corner, strides up and down. She says, "*Nobody* ever slapped me in my whole life! Not even my father when I was a little girl!" She touches her slightly reddened cheek, says, "Who does he think he is? Just because he's rich and wants to be Dru Resnik's producer, the son of a bitch!"

I put a hand on her shoulder, say, "Relax." But I'm too relieved to be truly sympathetic; I can't summon sympathy. She leans against me, sobs softly. She moves away almost at once, dries the corners of her eyes; she goes to check her face in the bathroom mirror.

I sit on the bed, try to think. I only hope that Nesbitt won't come here and try to make peace. From the bathroom, Elaine says, "Do you mind if I sleep here?"

I say, "No, of course not" in the most casual tone I can find. But I have no desire to be the consultant now or the consoler; my eyes hurt; it's after three. I take a sip of water from the jug: revolting. I turn off the light, lie flat on the bed.

Elaine takes her bag, digs in it, undresses, and puts on a nightgown; she turns off the bathroom light also, goes and slips into the other bed.

We are quiet and motionless for a few minutes, lying parallel, four feet apart. There are little sounds from outside, the very faint rustle of the evaporating water. Elaine says, "It's much better for it to end like this." But she's obviously sorry, in spite of her anger and her pretended detachment.

I turn toward her, say, "Why don't you come over here?"

She considers it for a moment; she slips out of the bed, pushes it beside mine, gets back under the sheets. I reach out one hand, graze a smooth shoulder. She turns on her side, says, "He always wants to *possess* everything he has to deal with; it's the only way he can feel secure."

153

"Terrible," I say; aware that she is practically in my bed, I can take my time.

She says, "And he doesn't realize that what's happening is a hundred times more important than his jealousy."

For a moment I think she's talking about us, and I'm surprised; I say, "Really?"

"It's not the voice of a physical person," she says. "It comes from above. It's chosen us so we can make a film with Dru that will change the way people look at the world and life and everything. We've been so incredibly lucky, but Jack doesn't realize, because basically he's weak and afraid."

Her voice is so lacking in a sense of humor that I'm glad we're in the dark; and she's so pathetic, thinking she could ever make a film "with" Dru. I say to her, "What do you mean, from above?"

"From above," she says. She hugs her legs, says, "Call it God, if you like."

I say to her, "Oh, come on"; I try to touch her hair.

"Dru's understood that, too," she says. "He's understood that You will give him the greatest inspiration he's ever had."

I say, *"Me?"*

"You, the spirit," Elaine says, losing her patience. *"You* will give him the inspiration to make an incredible film; compared to it, all the others will look like little amateurish videos, and when people see it, they'll understand the message and change their way of living and everything."

I say to her, "Really?" We are now so close, I can almost graze her leg with my leg.

She says, "A contact like this happens once every hundred years, or two hundred."

I touch her hip lightly with my fingers, sense a barely perceptible shudder. I lift the sheet, move closer, let my hand slip down to her thigh, stroke behind a knee, run my finger over the tender underside of a thigh; she stops my wrist, says, "We can't."

"Why not?" I say. I lean over to kiss her on one ear.

She sits up, says, "Because I'm a spiritual girl, and we're here on a mission." Her voice doesn't correspond much to her words, it's hard to figure out. She lies down, changes position two or three times, makes the springs creak.

I stretch out one hand again, very slowly; I take a few minutes to touch her hair, her throat. She moves closer, she sucks my shoulder, bites. She scratches my hip with her fingernails, moves down slowly to breathe on my stomach; she stops, says, "It's wrong, Dave. Tomorrow we have to receive enlightenment in the positive place; we can't do this." She moves away, turns over, but in the next moment turns back to me, closer.

We go on like this I don't know how long. It's a kind of ridiculous, confused torture; it's not doing us much good. We move in fits, sweating, our legs incredibly nervous, tangled in the sheets of the two sagging beds, and it's clear that whoever the voice is and whatever he wants, we're involved in a game conducted by others, and there's no way we can get out of it on our own. I don't give a damn anymore, I allow myself to sink down to the depths of sleep.

So we have allowed ourselves

So we have allowed ourselves to sink deeply into this story, and now it's hard to form any clear idea of what's happening, of the possible causes and consequences, to distinguish what corresponds to a plan and what, on the contrary, comes from mistakes and misconceptions and personal flaws. Hard to know if I am imagining more layers than there are, or if, on the contrary, there are more layers than I can imagine. If, for example, I would like to be with Elaine only because she's gone to Dave, or if she's gone to Dave so that I will want her here. If this threat to the equilibrium of our quartet is only a side effect, or, instead, a stimulus or a test. If we should go with the flow of things, as I've done so far, or try to oppose it, as Jack tends to do. Or if, in both cases, our reactions could be part of a plan that anticipates every little variable that we are able to produce. And the aim of all this isn't clear, not in the least; even if we choose to believe in it, it isn't clear. Are we here on a treasure hunt or a spiritual tour, or a business trip to convince me to put into my work elements different from those I generally use? I don't think I'm cut out to be the translator or disseminator of other people's messages. I'm not the director best suited to put together a film with a mission, however inspiring and noble and ordained it might be. I imagine that You knew this from the beginning, since You is so good at reading people's minds and foreseeing reactions and attitudes and moves. But this, too, is probably part of the system of contradictions that You has put together so carefully or so carelessly.

I don't know. I don't know what to expect from the positive place tomorrow: whether I'll walk away from it with my head full of intuitions that can be transformed into masterpieces of wisdom whenever I like, or whether I'll acquire a perspective so lofty and crystalline that it will make me lose interest completely in my work, make me see it as a simple conveyance, of no use anymore, a boat that has no importance once it has reached shore. Or perhaps I will be filled with disappointment and embarrassment at having believed in this possibility, even though I believed fitfully, with reservations and retreats and half-steps forward.

This is the sort of night that comes rarely, full of faint glints of distant attractions; it isn't a night for sleeping.

There's a knock at the door

There's a knock at the door; Dru's voice says, "Get moving; it's late!" The cabin is already filled with threads of light from all the cracks in the wood, the slats of the blinds. Elaine slips out of the bed without saying anything to me, collects her clothes and the bag, disappears into the bathroom.

Dru is outside, his hands in his pockets, his bag at his feet; he's eager to leave. He looks at his watch, looks at the half-closed door of my cabin. Elaine comes out, dressed in yet another combination of white; she kisses him on both cheeks. Dru looks at his watch again, says, "I hope Jack has finished his swim."

We go to put the bags in the jeep. Elaine stays out of reach, acts as if nothing had happened. She yawns, looks around as if sorry to have to leave so soon. Dru takes her by the arm, asks her something I can't hear, about the positive place. She thinks for a moment, says, "That could be." She bends down to collect a coconut still in its husk, says, "How do you open these things?"

"I don't know," Dru says, surprised, I believe, by her superficiality.

To regain ground, she says, "We must keep it for good luck." She puts the coconut in the jeep.

Dru and I go to the beach to call Jack. He's about fifteen yards from the shore, swimming froglike in the shallow water, his head well up to watch out for barracudas or other possible dangers. He comes toward us as soon as he sees us, stands up, walks through the water in slow strides for the last stretch. I'm unsure whether I should apologize or offer some explanation for last night; I try to stay behind Dru.

Dru looks at the palms and the beach, the crystalline water. He says, "Maybe if they'd sent us up some mountain covered with snow, it would all have been simpler."

We head for Atsantil along the sun-baked road that seems to quiver on the horizon. Elaine spreads suntan cream from a tube she brought from the hotel in Cancún; she passes it around. We don't encounter anyone, drive straight on between the two walls of vegetation. Elaine points up, says, "The hawk." But it's a crow; there are three others wheeling above us. Dru looks at them through narrowed eyes.

Finally there are two signs, and Nesbitt slows down, turns into a parking lot of packed earth. And it is even worse than Tis Talan: more cluttered with buses and cars and tourist groups and shoals of people; running motors, noises, smells, movement. There is an entire row of souvenir stands over-

flowing with rugs and ceramics and ponchos and cloth don-
keys and Kodak film and semiprecious stones and belts. We
sit in the jeep for at least one minute before getting out. We
had imagined a different antithesis, a place uncontaminated
and hidden, only for us.

Dru says, "All right"; he jumps down. Now that we aren't
moving, the sun is almost unbearable. We take a few steps
through the dust, turn back toward one of the stands; we buy
four broad-brimmed straw hats. Elaine says we have to buy
a camera, to record the images in this place so we can see
them again afterward. Dru says she's right; by now he has
become accustomed to the off-again, on-again nature of her
spiritual attitude, to the idea of not bothering to listen to her
one moment and taking her as gospel the next. Nesbitt bar-
gains with the souvenir vendor, buys an Instamatic and three
film cartridges for an incredible amount.

We fall in behind a long line of tourists a few yards beyond
the lot. The passage, uphill, is narrow; we proceed slowly
because of the friction with the opposite line of people returning. Dru looks puzzled; he flattens so as not to brush against
the yelling and giggling tourists; he slips past the stones of the
portal. Elaine and Nesbitt and I slip in after him; we take a
few steps, dazzled by the sun.

And maybe once again it's pure hypnotic suggestion, or a
reaction to our disappointment of two minutes ago, but all
four of us are impressed. Before us is a kind of little city,
sparse and irregular on the undulations of a pale-green
meadow, beyond which the ocean can be seen. But the city
is made of structures so incredibly *humble* compared to those
of Tis Talan. There is no great column, no impressive façade
or array of monoliths, no perfectly squared-off corner or perfectly erect wall. They are little more than houses, ancient,

accessible; you can imagine the paths going from one to another, as if exchanging looks or talk. Everything is arranged in a casual way, every little temple has a different orientation, facing the sun, the sea, the meadow. The equilibrium of the stones seems temporary, as if in the course of the night someone could come and pull a couple of buildings closer together, or move them apart, or even dismantle them to use their material differently. At the same time, the whole is curiously strong, not having to overcome great pressures or resistance.

None of us says anything; we follow Dru, who walks as if in a minefield. We climb up and down, following the undulation of the meadow. The relation between the temples changes; one is higher than the others; ten paces later, they are all on the same level; fifteen paces later, another rises above them all. The meadow is made of little leaves, round and flat, which probably don't need to be mowed; there are short palm trees, bushes at some distance from one another or grouped in the wildest way; vines cover and hide walls.

The other strange thing is that the tourists move and stop around the temples in shoals and herds that are not at all irksome. The tourists are not made insignificant by the imposing ferocity of buildings or by the enormity of empty space, as at Tis Talan; the movements and sounds here are absorbed by the landscape, purified without the knowledge of those who produce them. It doesn't even seem to be hot anymore, though the sun is at its peak and the light is extraordinarily intense.

We walk toward a little temple that now seems to be in the highest position. A guide is pointing it out to a circle of tourists, but we can't hear what he is saying. Some people are seated on its steps, on the flat, smooth stones around a kind of room at its summit. From above you can get a good view of the meadow and its buildings; of the shore on the other side, sloping sharply to the ocean. Elaine photographs me and Dru and Nesbitt, alone and then together; she asks a tourist to take some pictures of all of us and comes and poses in the center of the frame. We four smile as if we hadn't a problem in the world, as if we were fond of each other to exactly the same degree. Nesbitt puts an arm around my shoulder, gives me a friendly tap, tilts my hat. I no longer feel the least bit guilty toward him, or jealous of Elaine, who leans to give Dru a kiss. It seems to me I haven't been this euphoric many times in my life, this well-disposed. Dru smiles, says, "Isn't it incredible?"

We come down, walk aimlessly. Elaine keeps snapping pictures with her camera: she runs ahead and kneels, takes us from below and in profile, circles around us. She photographs the bushes, the meadow, the temples. We walk like an affectionate family, close and almost in contact, and a moment later we are each on his own, each lost.

My euphoria vanishes in a second; I stand, feeling the panic rising within me; I start running, I cut across a group of tourists, I look around frantically, my heart pounding. I don't know what it is; at this point it's not easy to be analytical. I run along behind a low wall, stumble, sprawl on the ground, pick myself up. But there's Elaine a few paces away, photographing a stone. I rush to her, grab her by one arm. She says, "Where the hell did everybody disappear to?"

I stick to her side, and a part of the spirit of last night returns, but even less defined, if that were possible. We walk among the tourists without saying anything or looking for Dru or Nesbitt; we sit on the stones of a temple. We breathe slowly, look around like simply structured animals. I seem to see everything from a parallel dimension now, protected by an opaque screen of well-being.

A man and a woman, perhaps on their honeymoon, keep climbing up and down the steps in front of us, as if trying to establish an impossible contact. They laugh and give each other little shoves and tugs, but I seem to understand that they are desperate. Elaine clutches my fingers every time the couple comes down, every time they sit again. We are inside the scene and outside it at the same time.

Then I hear a shout of "Daaaaaave!" and it's Dru and Nesbitt about a hundred yards away, making furious gestures. Elaine stands up at once, goes toward them. I follow her, full of resentment at this intrusion, this irreparable laceration of the atmosphere.

Dru says, "We've been looking for you two for an hour." He's irritated, far from the euphoria of the moment when we were all together on the temple.

Nesbitt shows us a piece of paper, says, "It was on the windshield of the jeep."

It says: *You will again be in the city of Los Angeles at ten o'clock tonight. You will meet the physical girl, and the following night all will be clarified. We are assisting you.*

Elaine tries to reread it more carefully. Dru says to her, "You can study it on the way," prodding her toward the exit. In the parking lot, too, he hurries us; he says, "The plane leaves in three hours!"

We get into the jeep like a commando team; Nesbitt drives off with a jerk, covers a group of tourists with dust.

But after ten minutes on the straight, empty road we are going at exactly the same speed as when we came, slowed down by the old engine and by the sun, by the lack of shadow and of reference points. Dru also seems to have forgotten he's in a hurry; he turns to one side, sticks his legs out, as if from a boat. Nesbitt constantly adjusts the string of his straw hat; he slows down a couple of times to fix it more securely. Elaine keeps her face turned into the sun, her chin raised, her eyes closed. We advance out of sheer power of inertia, without a thought in our heads.

Then we are at the broad curve just before the airport; we straighten in our seats, make an effort to be frenzied again. Nesbitt brakes in front of the doors; we jump down with our bags, run inside, across the lounge, and learn that the plane to Los Angeles left almost an hour ago. Dru looks around, full of anger, says, "How the hell is that possible?"

We try the desks of all the airlines; all the clerks shake their heads in the same way, saying there are no more flights for the States until tomorrow morning. Dru says, "This is ridiculous"; he insists until they begin to be annoyed.

Nesbitt also tries asking; he speaks with a uniformed man who looks at him with indifferent eyes. He comes back to us, says, "Nothing doing." This business must have sapped him, because he moves much less confidently than on the evening he came to pick up me and Dru in Los Angeles; his eyes are ten times more puzzled. Elaine doesn't do much to help; she puts her bag on top of mine, sits on them.

Dru is exasperated; he says to me, "Dave, see if you can find some lousy private plane or something. There *has* to be a way to get out of this place." Now he's using the tone he uses on the set, as if he were held up by some stupid confusion in the midst of shooting a scene.

I go and ask at the tourist information desk; the girl says to try at the car rentals desk. The Hertz boy points dubiously at the Avis boy; the Avis boy at the Budget boy. The Budget boy scratches his neck, says, "Come with me a minute." I follow him through a door in a prefabricated panel of the wall, outside onto the dry grass before the runway, up some metal steps that lead to a concrete cube.

Inside, there's a character with a crew cut sitting behind a desk. The Budget boy explains rapidly that I want to hire a plane; the character looks at my shoes, says: "To go where?" I say, "Los Angeles." He stares at me for a moment; he laughs, baring yellow teeth, a purplish tongue. For the rest, he is very neat, in a Glen-plaid jacket and a thin striped shirt. The Budget boy also laughs, but he doesn't seem very pleased; he opens the door again. I follow him down the steps, into the airport. He goes back to his desk, not saying anything further.

I explain to Dru that the pilot burst out laughing. He says, "But he has a plane, doesn't he?" He goes to the door I just came through.

Nesbitt and Elaine and I follow him outside. The pilot is locking up the concrete cube; he turns to look down at us. From below, Dru says to him, "We go United States." He makes a gesture to indicate the United States.

The pilot laughs again, says, "My plane too little!" He makes a reductive gesture, holding his hands close.

Dru waves one arm in an arc, says, "Enough take us bigger airport." He extends his arms to indicate bigger. He says, "Pay much. Many dollars." He rubs his index finger and thumb together to indicate dollars.

The pilot looks down at us from the top of the steps, shakes his head. Nesbitt says in a low voice, "We don't even know if he can fly. . . ."

But the pilot suddenly changes his mind, says, "Okay, okay. I take you Mérida. Then from Mérida, United States: Pan Am. Aeromexico. Eastern. Continental. Mexicana. Eh?"

"From Mérida we have to take a scheduled flight," Elaine says in the tone of a simultaneous translator.

"I got that," Dru says. "So long as we get moving."

We wait for the pilot to take something from the concrete cube and come down the steps; we follow him on the searing tarmac. He points to a little red-and-white twin-engine at the edge of the runway, made even smaller by a DC-10 parked nearby. Nesbitt and I run to collect the bags.

We all pile inside; I'm pressed at the rear, Dru and Nesbitt in the middle, Elaine beside the pilot. The pilot starts the engines, adjusts his jacket. The plane isn't in tip-top condition, judging by the way it shakes even before we begin to move. Nesbitt tightens the seat belt, huffs. The pilot fiddles with switches and dials, says something into the radio; he makes a couple of rickety curves on the runway and then drives straight ahead, picking up speed. We shake madly; the noise is unbelievable. Dru hangs on to his seat, avoids looking out.

We're in the air, and the cockpit is shaking so hard, it seems about to fall to pieces. We climb in fits and starts, the wing dipping, the plane rearing, as the engines growl furiously. We gain altitude very slowly; it's likely that we are well over the maximum load. After maybe ten minutes we stop climbing and level out, and immediately there is an air pocket or something; we drop, all of us with terrified faces. The pilot recoups ably, carries us to our proper altitude again. He turns and looks at us, shouts, "Stop being so tense! You think you've come all the way up here just to crash?" He shouts this in perfectly articulated English, with no trace of the pidgin he was using at the airport. Dru looks at him, unable to speak.

And it's strange, because we continue dropping and recovering worse than ever, but nobody is the least worried anymore. It becomes a kind of roller-coaster ride, where the dips and the vibrations and the noise are part of the fun, enhanced by the altitude and by the sun beating through the windows, by the view of the green expanse below. It seems a perfectly safe game, as if we were masters of the air and of the force of gravity, of distance vertical and horizontal. We laugh every time the plane falls, we look out the windows at the approaching forest. The pilot yells, "Come on! Come on!" and pretends he's unable to regain altitude. He looks at Elaine from time to time and teases her, dips one wing, then the other, as if losing control. Elaine laughs, screams at him, "Stop it!" Dru shakes Nesbitt by one shoulder, yells, "Are you taking all this in, Yellow?" I don't think he's ever in his life flown in this kind of mood; Nesbitt nods his head.

Then the pilot points below to the gray of the Mérida airport; he begins to descend. As we go down in jerks to the runway, Dru stretches toward him, shouts to him, "Did you know in advance that you'd have to bring us here?"

The pilot yells, "What?" We touch the tarmac gracelessly, bouncing a few hundred yards before stopping.

We sit still in our places; the pilot taps two fingers on his watch; he says, "You run or miss next flight too."

We get out, Nesbitt pays, Dru continues to look at the pilot until Elaine pulls him away. We run to the airport building, enter just as they are removing from the board the card for the only flight to Los Angeles. We go through check-in and customs like lunatics, run outside and up the steps of the 727 a moment before the steps are rolled away.

In Los Angeles it is exactly ten o'clock

In Los Angeles it is exactly ten o'clock when we step out onto the sidewalk in front of the airport, with our Mexican hats hanging down our backs, like four returning tourists. We all look at our watches, but at this point it is hard for us to be amazed.

Nesbitt takes us back to the hotel; he drives in silence. His expression is that of a child who has discovered something upsetting about his parents. He says good-bye to us under the marquee, says he's going home for a shower and he'll join us later to see what happens with the physical girl. Elaine stays with us; she crosses the lobby with her knowing stride.

Dru talks with all three of the desk clerks, but there are no messages, no phone calls have arrived, no letters or anything. Two workmen in overalls are unrolling a cable along one wall,

168

under the supervision of a fat character; there are people coming in, people leaving, people talking on the phone, as always.

In the elevator Elaine barely glances at me, as if last night had been shelved and forgotten for centuries. In the corridor I try to get next to her to ask her if she wants to come to my room to rest or have a shower or something like that, but she walks straight on, slips into Dru's room as soon as he opens the door. Dru says, "We'll meet in twenty minutes"; he closes the door in my face.

I remain in the corridor a few seconds, go to my room so infuriated and jealous that my fingers slip on the shower knob; I can't even regulate the temperature. It's incredible the way Elaine can be so cynical and superficial and indifferent: it's ridiculous that the voice should call her the spiritual girl. But Dru also fills me with rage, by his way of taking everything as his due, not giving a moment's thought to the feelings of others, except when he needs them for atmosphere. I feel like going to his room and kicking the door, asking Elaine at least to tell me what's going on in her head.

I go downstairs and find them sitting in the lobby in a detached manner, Dru dressed semiformally, Elaine in a little white suit that allows full view of her trim legs. Dru says, "Jack called. He was too exhausted, he's gone to bed."

"And the physical girl?" I say. It would be an improvement if there were another girl; I don't believe Dru is interested in Elaine in any specific way.

He stands up, says, "I don't know. They didn't explain who she is or how she will arrive."

"We shouldn't worry about that," Elaine says in a hit-or-miss attempt at the spiritual tone. "In the note, You says all will be clarified."

It is eleven-thirty, and the only restaurant in the hotel still open is the Hawaiian place downstairs. We go there without any appetite, and even though it's again almost empty, the maître d' takes us to the same table where we sat with Camado the night before he disappeared. Dru makes a strange face when he realizes this; he looks around.

We order as little as possible; we study the glasses, shift them a fraction of an inch. I try to intercept Elaine's gaze, but she is paying attention only to Dru; she makes a few totally vacuous remarks on the possible role of the physical girl. Dru hardly listens to her, pours himself some water. The dim lights only make the atmosphere worse.

Then I look up and there's Rickie coming toward us. She's wearing a dinner jacket with no blouse underneath, black tights, her hair cut in a shorter bob than last time. She smiles, embraces and kisses all three of us, takes a seat. She says, "I was at a party at Redondo Beach; it took me *hours* to get here."

"But how did you know we were back?" Dru says. He's genuinely surprised; he continues staring at her.

"I knew," Rickie says, shrugs.

Dru smiles with wonder; he no longer even looks at Elaine, on his left. Elaine leans forward so as not to be excluded, and she seems slightly less beautiful than five minutes ago: with thinner lips, smaller eyes.

We are silent for a few minutes; nobody is able to use any of the subjects of conversation that lie within our reach. The waiter arrives with the dishes; we push them aside as soon as he leaves.

Dru says to Rickie, "You has said we'd meet this evening and tomorrow night everything will be clarified, but he didn't explain what happens in the meanwhile."

"The spirit, You?" Rickie says with an agreeable, slightly didactic look.

"Yes," Dru says. Elaine is still all over him; even though it's clear he's attracted to Rickie, surprised by her expressions.

Rickie says, "Something physical has to happen between me and the colors, I believe."

Elaine now gives her a venomous look, the way a middle-aged, middle-class woman might look at an uncontrollable girl trying to steal her husband.

Dru takes a long sip from his glass. A lot of it may be fatigue, but he definitely has an embarrassed expression. He says, "How do you mean, physical?" He is so interested in her that if Elaine weren't as insensitive as she is, there would be no problem: we could be perfectly satisfied, all four of us.

Rickie laughs, says, "Now, let's see." She points a finger at me, says, "For example, Dave and I now could go on up."

Dru is disappointed; Elaine, full of relief. I say, "But why, after all?" I don't have the least desire to remain stuck with her while Dru takes Elaine to bed, and, what's more, does so reluctantly. I say, "Can't you and Dru go instead, or else wait till tomorrow, when Nesbitt's well again?"

Rickie says, "It's a question of color combinations, Dave. Blue comes before green. Yellow isn't here at the moment, so it's as if it didn't exist."

"But how do you know?" I say. "Who told you?"

She smiles, looks down. She's fairly sexy, actually, in this dinner jacket with nothing underneath, this mellifluous and childish way of moving. What I can't bear is for somebody to arrange situations for me from outside, whoever it is and whatever grand plan they may have in mind. I look at Elaine, but instead of helping me, she says, "Da-ave."

Dru says, "Dave, for days now we've been following the instructions and doing whatever they ask us; should we spoil everything now?"

"It's not a question of spoiling things," I say.

"Let's go, then," Rickie says, in high spirits.

Dru and Elaine also consider my resistance overcome; they stand up. The waiter points at the untouched plates, asks if there was anything wrong. Dru says to him, "No, no," signs the check.

We go up to our floor without any further talk. Rickie's tights couldn't fit her better; her legs couldn't be more shapely; Dru stays a few paces behind her in the corridor to watch her walk. She turns around a couple of times, laughs. Dru stops at his door, says, "We'll all meet tomorrow."

Elaine accompanies me and Rickie into my room with the attitude of a social worker. She looks at me reassuringly, says, "It's all positive; don't worry."

"I'm not worried," I say.

She says, "Good night, you two," closes the door.

Rickie takes off her shoes with the greatest naturalness, goes into the bathroom to pee, wash her face. She moves about the room as if it were hers, or at least as if she had spent several weeks in it. She sits down at the little table, takes from the pockets of her dinner jacket a pouch of marijuana and her pipe; she begins to fill it. I walk back and forth, turn on some music: an old Paul McCartney song in an arrangement full of saccharine violins. I try to turn it up, but it won't go beyond a certain volume. I go to the door, unlock it, lock it. This is a ridiculous situation; the only other time we saw each other, she was entirely directed at Dru, as if I weren't even there. And we're not borne on the wave of any impulse, gripped by any eagerness to communicate. She turns, says, "Why are you so tense, Dave?"

"I'm not tense," I say. I fiddle with the controls of the air-conditioning; I say, "I mean, we haven't even *talked* to each other."

She lights the pipe, inhales deeply. She says, "We're only following the instructions"; she blows out the smoke a little at a time.

I say, "Yes, but at least I'd like to know the *aim* of these instructions, and exactly where they come from." I sit on the bed, say, "I'm not all that mystical, by inclination."

She smiles, takes another drag on the pipe. Then she comes and slips the bedspread from beneath me, lays it out on the carpet at the foot of the bed. She turns off the main light, leaves a little lamp on, says, "Take off your jacket and sit here."

Now the whole thing irritates me even more; she has this almost professional tone. I say to her, "Wait a minute, goddammit. Can't we talk for a minute, at least?"

She sits on the bedspread with her legs crossed, smiles patiently. She says, "What would you like to talk about?"

I take off my jacket, go and sit down facing her. I say, "What I don't understand . . . "

She doesn't even listen to me; she puts her hand on my temples, says, "Close your eyes and breathe deeply."

I close my eyes. She puts her thumbs on them, without pressing much. I inhale her smell: the resinous aroma of marijuana mixed with the perfume she put on before leaving home mixed with the odors she collected at the party she went to. She says, "Now I want you to think very intensely about the first period of history that comes into your mind, and try to form a clear image of what you see."

I try, but the only image that comes to me is her sitting opposite me at the moment when she asked me to close my eyes. I say, "Nothing."

She massages my temples and eyelids, barely moves her fingers. She says, "Try again."

I make an effort; some illustrations from the *National Geographic* go through my head, some snatches of costume films: people in a market dressed like Egyptian extras, with tunics and sandals, et cetera.

Rickie says, "Tell me what you see." She breathes close to me, transmits warmth. Rather than disappoint her, I say, "People in a market, near some big walls." I'm not even sure about the walls; maybe I'm only trying to add background.

She says, "Yes, yes." She presses harder now, her fingertips sweating slightly. She says, "How are they dressed? Try to describe them."

"Tunics," I say. "Sort of Egyptian tunics." The scene I have in mind is always the same; I can't manage to shift the point of view or make anything happen. I believe it's a scene from a film: I can't remember which one. I say, "I don't see much."

Rickie says, "No, that's right. It's perfect!"

I reopen my eyes: she's in the same position as when I closed them, but so excited and flushed that I lean forward to give her a kiss, try to reach her lips. She quickly moves aside, makes me fall on my face, she presses her hands on my back. She tries to slip off my shirt but can't manage; she says, "Take it off."

I take off my shirt; she crushes me on the bedspread, straddles my back. I try to wriggle free, but she's fairly heavy and strong; she presses her knees, begins massaging the base of my neck. She has real technique; she works on the muscles in circular movements, with energy. It isn't unpleasant; I feel her physical current passing through me. She proceeds with a rhythm that accelerates little by little, completely concentrated.

Then she takes off the dinner jacket, flings it aside. I see her full breasts for a moment, before she flattens me again, resumes massaging my back. She is breathing behind my ears now, grazing my skin with hers. I turn and I hold her around the shoulders, pull her up to lip contact. She resists and then lets herself go, falls against me; we kiss, roll to one side. She is warm and smooth, incredibly substantial compared to Elaine last night. I slip off her black tights, and underneath she isn't wearing anything. I run my fingers over her compact surface with a kind of uncontrollable delight. She has a breathy laugh, widens her legs, pulls me toward her. She has a generosity without apparent limits; there doesn't seem to be the slightest shadow between her thoughts and her body. It occurs to me again that whoever organized all this must have wanted to play with antithesis; but I can't think about it much, I'm too involved in her extraordinary, elastic fullness. I am magnetized, attracted, overwhelmed; it's useless to put up any resistance.

I take maybe five minutes to catch my breath. I slide closer to her again, give her some kisses on the cheekbones, on the forehead. With her eyes closed, she smiles, more at herself than at me, I think. I shake her, hoping that some more direct expression will come from her. She opens her eyes, says, "What is it?"

I look at her face, very close, and inside I feel rising a possessive alarm, Nesbitt-like. It comes from the stomach, reaches the heart and then the head, all in the space of a second. I say to her, "Rickie. Just try to explain it to me for a moment."

She looks at me as you might look at a poor hypersensitive child; she says, "What?"

"Us," I say. I don't think I've ever been so full of anxiety with a girl in my whole life. She seems so self-sufficient, so unattainable, even though she's here, only a few inches away. I say, "What happened just now. I mean, is it only because of You's instructions and the business with the colors?"

She says, "What do you think?" She puts on my shirt, goes to collect her marijuana pipe.

To see her at a slight distance makes my apprehension greater; I say to her, "I did it only because I like you." I don't give a damn about revealing myself like this; I stand up, say to her, "Because I like you *a lot*."

"I like you, too," she says in an entirely neutral tone. She sits down again with her legs crossed, lights the pipe, inhales.

I tear it from her, say, "Let me have a drag, too," to get her attention. I take a couple of drags, cough. The situation only worsens; I become so apprehensive and possessive that I can no longer keep still. I clasp her by the wrist, say, "And now what happens? With the business of the combinations of colors and green coming after blue and all the rest? What does it mean?" I imagine Dru waiting in his room, entertained by Elaine, who's doing *I Ching* for him or paying him compliments, jealous but also resigned to the idea of Rickie arriving at any moment.

Rickie reaches over and sets the pipe on the coffee table; my shirt doesn't cover her behind. She says, "In a little while I'll go next door. Elaine can come to you."

"I don't give a damn about Elaine," I say. I put my pants back on; I can't stand being naked while she is wearing my shirt and saying she's going to Dru. I say, "You're not going anywhere. You're staying here."

She looks at me with an expression of such surprise that my apprehension degenerates into sheer anguish. She says, "Dave, if it wasn't for You and his voice, the two of us would never have been together."

176

"That's not so," I say. I grab her shoulders, say, "Anyway, there's no sense in saying it, because at this point we *have* been together."

She doesn't try to free herself, even though she could without much effort. She half closes her eyes, and it's clear I don't have a chance in this world of convincing her to stay.

I let go of her, move to the door, full of hatred for this bastard You who interferes in people's private lives to perform experiments in emotional chemistry, hatred for Rickie's dumb faith as sacrificial lamb, Dru's vicious and purposeful curiosity. I open the door, say, "I'm going down to get some mineral water." Rickie says something to me, but I'm already outside, already hurrying down the corridor.

I move with extraordinary ease, glide along more than run; I barely have time to see a spot and I'm already past it. I slide by the doors, to the elevator, but I don't feel like waiting, so it's down flights and flights of service stairways and through the lobby. My euphoria at this fluidity of motion compensates for my few moments of possessive anger; I am halfway across the lobby before I realize that I have nothing on except my pants. I slide to the opposite wall, flatten against some wood paneling. There are a few people at a great distance, too taken up with their nighttime activities to notice me. I slip to one of the many telephones, to the refuge of a pale-blue half-shell. I check the space from here, with a kind of insect vision, it seems to me. There is an Iranian at a telephone four or five shells farther along; he looks at my bare feet but doesn't change his expression. I turn the other way, make some mental tests of a possible semielectronic voice on the basis of how Dru described it; a possible semielectronic sentence saying that the physical girl must stay with me. I call Dru's number, but it's busy. I try again. The Iranian goes on staring at my feet; I hide one behind the other. I try the number again: busy. It occurs to me that maybe Rickie has already gone next door, that Dru has unplugged the phone and is already having an orgy without even sending me Elaine, since I'm not there. It occurs to me that instead of running out like a fool I should have stayed in my room and kept the door shut. I cross the lobby with long leaps, slip into an elevator just as an elderly couple is entering it.

They also look at my feet; they turn away, act as if nothing were happening. I press the button for my floor a couple of times, tap my finger on it still as we are going up. I am again overwhelmed by apprehension. This must be one of the slowest elevators in the world; it takes hours to go four floors. The couple look at the luminous numbers, tilting their heads as if they had a whole lifetime at their disposal for getting back to their room.

Then finally I'm at the right floor, but the corridor is much longer than I remembered it, with dozens and dozens of identical doors. I go forward in starts and stops between one door and the next, my heart pounding, until I find my door. I knock like a madman, fiddle with the knob. Rickie comes and opens, still wearing my shirt; she says, "Where's the water?"

I lock the door, turning the key five times; I put on the chain, go and unplug the phone.

"What are you doing?" Rickie says, but without great interest. She turns on the TV, watches it, kneeling a few inches away. I go and hug her from behind, press my hands on her breasts. She turns her head to kiss me: a deep and wet and indifferent kiss, like a great herbivore's. Slowly I raise the shirt. There's a knocking at the door. Rickie frees herself, goes and opens it. I lean against the TV stand, let myself slide to the ground.

Elaine comes in, her hair tousled, her eyes red. She looks at the bed, the rumpled bedspread, me on the floor. She says, "You two have to stay here together. You's called and he said that at this moment our equilibriums are perfect and we mustn't break them."

Rickie nods her head, turns to look at me. It seems to me there is a touch of disappointment in her naturalness, but it's hard to be sure.

Elaine walks around on tiptoe, says, "He explained a lot of things to us, things we have to do tomorrow; Dru will tell you. Tomorrow night everything will be clarified." She goes back to the door, says "Good night," leaves. It's incredible the way I don't give a damn about her anymore.

Rickie takes off the shirt, slips into the bed. I go and sit down beside her, look into her eyes; I say, "Are you glad to stay here, or not?" She doesn't even answer me, pulls aside the covers so I can climb in.

Rickie opens the curtain

Rickie opens the curtain, lets every corner of the room fill with light. She steps out to look at the patio with the pool; she says, "I'm going down for a swim."

I say to her, "Wait for me"; I get out of the bed, still half asleep, slip on something while she brushes her teeth with the greatest precision.

At the patio, we go to the swimming-articles stand; I tell her to pick out whatever she wants. The sun makes my eyes hurt; it hasn't been a restful night, or a long one. Rickie bends down to look through the glass; she points at the suit and the cap and the goggles that cost most. I show the salesgirl the key to my room, tell her to put everything on the bill. Rickie seems pleased, smiles at me as she goes off to change.

I wait for her by the water, nervous again, thinking that she could have gone off God knows where. But she comes out of the dressing room, wearing the black, professional suit and the cap that makes her head smaller; she walks toward me like a kind of Olympic divinity. In the artificial light of the room I hadn't realized she was perfect in such a disturbing, almost unnatural way. Just seeing her fills me with jealousy; I turn to check the two or three men lying in the sun.

She comes within two paces of me; she slips on the goggles, and it's as if she had thrust me away. She goes to one end of the pool, steps back, runs and dives; she slices below the surface of the water, glides like a seal to the other end of the tank. She emerges to catch her breath and is immediately off again, coming my way in a fast crawl. When she turns again, I also dive, and swim alongside her. I keep up with her for fifteen or twenty feet, then she begins to outdistance me even though I fight, arms and legs, as hard as I can, straining my muscles like a madman. I try to speed up, breathe faster; in convulsive fits I burn up all my reserves of energy, but it doesn't help, she's ahead of me, inexorable, by a length, two lengths; she leaves me splashing and making foam in her wake, short of breath, with my heart pounding. She swings around and comes back, passes me before I get to the end; she has lapped me already. I keep going for a few minutes, but give up even trying, uncertain in the water, like a beaten fish. I come out, watch her, slapping the water with my feet as she goes back and forth at the same impossible pace.

Finally she stops, puffs, clings to the edge; she pushes down, leaps out. She takes off the goggles and the cap, shakes her hair. She comes and gives me a shove, says "Lazybones," laughs.

We try calling Dru on the phone by the pool, but the line's

busy. We dress, go back upstairs. In the corridor there is a stocky man by the elevator; he follows us with his eyes. Rickie walks with a musical-comedy step, humming a little tune without words, only "Da-da-dats-dada." We stop at Dru's door: the DO NOT DISTURB sign is hanging on the knob. Rickie points a finger, covers her mouth with one hand.

In the room I watch her as she rinses the suit and cap and goggles in the basin, puts them in their little case, folds the case, and slips it into a pocket of her dinner jacket. It's incredible how she can perform these simple acts in such an energetic and precise way; I'm filled with admiration. Then she says, "I have to run home; I'll be back in about an hour."

Without much dignity or independence, I ask her, "Can I come, too?"

She looks at me for a moment, nods.

In the garage she has a BMW with a metallic finish, almost new. Into the stereo player she slips a cassette of the music she played for us at her house the night of the slide show: the distilled piano, familiar and alien. We drive along Wilshire; the sounds are perfectly suited to the flow of cars in broad daylight, to the bright outlines of the landscape. I look at her in profile as she puts on a pair of dark glassses, and I can't imagine how I could ever get any kind of hold on her.

She stops in her street behind a pink fifties Buick with long fins and little round taillights and excessive chrome. She runs one hand along its side, says, "It belongs to a friend of mine." Her apartment is more or less as I remembered it, with the lace curtains at the windows and the little Alpine landscapes on the walls. She taps the keys of her answering machine, takes off her shoes. She walks around as she listens to the messages, puts some objects in their proper place. A girl's recorded voice says, "Rickie, it's Britt, I've been trying to get you all morning, I have to go out now." A man's recorded voice says only, "Mel. I hope you haven't forgotten." Rickie says something to herself, barely moves her lips. There are two slide-holder sheets on the table, among newspaper clippings and little boxes of lacquered wood, makeup pencils. I look at them in the light from the window: Rickie, naked, in sexy poses on a big white bed with a brass frame. She says, "Tony Rico took those; Elaine knows him, too." She doesn't seem the least bit embarrassed, she picks up four or five color prints from the same series, throws them at me. They are stunning, but somehow their power is diminished by the poses and the makeup, by the standard expressions they made her assume. She is much more attractive now as she walks absently around the room barefoot, collecting things and throwing them from one corner to another.

I follow her into the bedroom, say to her, "You're much better the way you are."

She slips off the black tights, kicks them aside; she says, "I know, but you have to begin somewhere." She takes a short white skirt from a drawer, throws away the dinner jacket. I look at her as she slips on the skirt and a white jacket, smooths her hips. This bedroom is even neater and more childish than the rest of the house: it's a kind of little girl's dream of a bedroom, with photographs of her parents at either side of an oval mirror, a plush teddy bear on the bed, between two embroidered pillows. She examines herself a moment in the mirror, goes back to the living room to telephone.

The kitchen doesn't look much used; on the shelves there is only a bottle of wheat-germ oil; in the refrigerator, one fat-free yogurt. There are telephone numbers on an erasable board; a postcard from Aspen, Colorado, over the sink, with the words "Lots of kisses, Tom." But I am beyond jealousy now, I am too dazed.

Rickie clips her toenails as she talks over the phone, lifts one knee, then the other. There is a Japanese electric guitar propped in one corner; on the wall beside it, a photograph of her with the guitar. She says into the phone, "Yes, yes, I promise, I *promise*," hangs up, huffs. She looks at me for a moment, dials another number, but it's busy.

I say to her, "Do you play?" It's hard to make a connection, I don't know where to start.

She says, "Yes." She goes and gets her marijuana pipe, says to me, "Come outside."

We go out on the little terrace where she waved to us on the night of the slide show, we sit on a little wicker love seat. She smokes, again doesn't offer it to me. I ask her, "What do you do for a living?"

She blows out some bluish smoke. She stands up, walks along the edges of the terrace. She says, "I buy Mercedeses and BMWs in Germany and sell them here for five times as much." She seems very concrete and straightforward, but a second later she looks down at the street as if what she has just said hadn't the slightest meaning.

"What about the photographs?" I say. I look at her swimmer's legs as she bends to scratch one knee. I feel too rational and simple and attached to an existence that's normal compared to hers; I'm unfulfilled, lacking interest. And I wish the semielectronic voice wasn't mixed up in this, or Dru or Nesbitt, or films or money or anything else.

She closes her eyes, reopens them, says, "I'll recite you a poem of mine." She strikes a rhetorical pose, begins to recite verses. At the beginning I'm embarrassed for her; then some sounds and some images seem beautiful to me; then it occurs to me that this isn't a poem of hers at all, it's a song the Dire Straits did a few years ago. I tell her so; she does a turn, says, "I changed some words." She picks up the pipe again, slips into the house.

I stay on the love seat, without the energy to follow her; I stretch out on one side.

Rickie shakes me by the arm, says, "Hey, wake up!" She shows me her watch; it's four o'clock. I leap up, my head completely confused. We run out, jump into the car.

In the lobby of the hotel there are two or three men like the one who looked at us this morning; they are keeping an eye on the movement. The workmen in coveralls are still fiddling with cables, hooking up.

Rickie stops paying attention to me the minute we step out of the elevator; she heads straight for Dru's room. The door is ajar; she taps lightly, then goes in.

But Dru isn't there, or Elaine: there's a tall, wrinkled man about seventy, in an ugly brown suit, his hair almost shaved at the temples. A second, younger, man is rummaging in a suitcase; he freezes.

Rickie points to the door, says, "I thought this was room 457."

"This *is* room 457," the wrinkled man says. He's wearing glasses with a transparent frame, has a scratch on one cheekbone.

Rickie looks around, and there's a rift in her naturalness. She says, "Where is Mr. Resnik, then?"

"Don't ask *us,*" the younger man says. He is half bent over, full of compressed hostility.

Rickie steps backward toward me, says in a whisper, "Let's get out of here."

We slip outside, go along the corridor. A voice behind us shouts, "Where the hell are you running to?"

We turn: Dru is looking out from the door opposite the one we entered; he says, "It's *half past four,* you irresponsible idiots!"

Rickie goes and hugs and kisses him; she enters the room and hugs and kisses Elaine and Nesbitt there. Elaine says, "We moved over here last night because *You* called and said we had to be on the north side."

Rickie sits on the bed, massages a calf. She asks, "What are the new instructions?"

Dru says, "Elaine will tell you"; he goes and looks out the window. He's not in a good mood at all, maybe because we came back so late, maybe because Rickie stayed with me, maybe because he's already fed up with Elaine.

Elaine assumes her best inspired pose, says, "Now then. First he said that now the two girls also have a color; I'm white and you, Rickie, are pink."

"How wonderful," Rickie says, in the tone of somebody who'd have preferred some other color.

Elaine says, "Then he said that the general situation is positive, that Jack has suffered but it was necessary to restore mobility to his feelings, which were blocked."

Nesbitt looks at the tip of one shoe, scrapes it over the carpet.

"Just explain what we have to do now," Dru says impatiently. "Otherwise we'll never get out of here."

Elaine looks for a compromise between speed and a still-acceptable tone of inspiration; she says, "We have to buy new clothes, each in his or her color. Then we have to buy musical instruments; it doesn't matter whether we can play them or not; we just have to decide which instrument we would really like and take that one. Then, at midnight, we have to be in this room with the new clothes and the instruments, and everything will be clarified through the music, or anyway the music is very important for the explanations that You has to give us."

Rickie absorbs the information as if she were at school, intent. Dru goes to the door, says, "Now let's go, or else the stores will all close. It's Saturday, goddammit."

We follow him downstairs in a hurry; he can infect everyone when he wants to. In the lobby Elaine says rapidly, "There's another color, gray, it's a girl who'll be with Jack, and in that way the nucleus will be complete and all the colors will be in perfect harmony at the moment of enlightenment." Nesbitt turns to look at the workmen in coveralls who are now setting up a velvet rope to keep back crowds, along a route from the entrance to the doors of the convention hall. The men keeping an eye on the movement remain in the background; other men and women, with big badges on their lapels, are moving closer to the plate glass.

Outside, we argue about what to buy first, clothes or instruments. The girls insist on clothes; they say there's a fantastic place nearby, they point at a big building with arcades visible beyond a parking lot. Dru says, "Let's get moving, then."

We walk rapidly along a narrow half-sidewalk not meant for pedestrians; we climb a ramp, cross the vast concrete expanse almost empty of cars at this hour. The place the girls named is a very pretentious, brightly lighted and luxurious department store, with counters of French perfume and fancy costume jewelry on the ground floor, crocodile handbags and wallets and belts and designer stockings. Elaine and Rickie are filled with excitement the moment we enter; they look around with shining eyes. At the first escalator, they dump us, say, "We'll meet you in a little while."

Dru and Nesbitt and I go down to the men's department, roam around, somewhat puzzled. The salesmen have carefully styled hair, are dressed in the same clothes they sell; they observe us from behind their counters without making the slightest offer to help us. We walk in a little formation for a few minutes, then Dru says, "Maybe it would be better for each of us to look for his color." We separate, go in different directions, without much enthusiasm.

The strange thing is that, if you consider it abstractly, it should be a dream, to choose whatever you want among clothes you could never afford on your own and then let Nesbitt foot the bill. But the more I proceed along the racks and shelves, the more the idea seems confused to me, beyond fulfillment. I try on three or four jackets, touch the fabric of maybe thirty others, but I don't have any criterion, instinctive or rational, which could help me reach a decision. I walk along the blond wood partitions, follow the rows of mannequins; I look at the shades of blue, pale or deep or matte, sky blue and cobalt blue, ultramarine, navy almost black, and I don't even stop. I drag myself along in this recycled air made even less breathable by this enormous quantity of woven fibers, and I no longer know the reason we came here. I walk faster; with claustrophobic eyes I hunt for the exit.

Behind a shelved corner there is Dru with a green wool jacket in his hand. He also looks extremely ill at ease; he says to me, "What do you think?" I tell him to try it on. He slips it on, but the size is ridiculous, and there are accordion pleats over the hips. He rips it off, says, "Lousy jacket!" I don't believe he often finds himself in a big department store to pick out clothes; for years a tailor has probably made everything to measure for him. He says, "If those two silly girls hadn't run upstairs like that. Go find them and tell Elaine to come down here; we need her advice."

I go up to the third floor, spend a good ten minutes wandering around before I find them. Naturally they've only just begun: each has various dresses over her arm; they are halfway between the racks and the dressing rooms. Elaine says, "We'll be down in five minutes," almost without looking at me. On her feet Rickie already has a pair of pink shoes with high heels that make her even showier; she doesn't even notice that I've come upstairs.

On the floor below, Dru is irritated the moment he sees me come back alone; he says, "What *children* those girls are, goddammit. The whole thing's only symbolic; we're not here to renew our wardrobe." I help him, ransack the whole floor in search of green jackets in shades and sizes that are at least acceptable. This is the classic task of an assistant now; I run back and forth with heavy jackets, picking out and taking back the wrong sizes, with Dru by the dressing rooms, saying, "Well?" Finally he looks at himself in the mirror with the best jacket I could find for him; he wears it in such a way that it appears revolting. He says, "Hmph." He isn't in a great preenlightenment mood, it seems to me.

To avoid irritating him further, I pick for myself the first blue jacket that comes to hand, take it along with his to the cash desk. This is a crime, too, but I feel nauseated at the mere idea of having to make a choice. We go and look for Nesbitt, see him walking along a rack; he reaches the end and turns around. He comes to us, says, "There's nothing yellow here. *Nothing.*"

We take a turn around the department together, ask a couple of salesmen, and in fact the only thing they have in yellow is a down jacket for mountain-climbing. Dru tries to persuade Nesbitt to take that at least, but Nesbitt won't hear of it. Dru says, "Let's go up and see if those two have finished, and we can look for another place before it's too late. We still have all the instruments to buy, for God's sake." He manages to make the bad general mood still worse; we run up the escalators, cross the women's department like three burglars.

Rickie is trying on a mauve belt at a mirror, with one hand on her hip and her head tilted. She says, "Do you think this could be considered pink?"

"Yes, yes," Dru says, furious. He says, "Where the hell's Elaine gone to?"

Rickie doesn't lose one bit of her composure; she says, "She must be somewhere around here." She takes off the belt, tries on another, which she had hung over a chrome bar.

Nesbitt and I run to look for Elaine; we cover the entire department, find her back where we started, as she is asking some final advice of Rickie, while Dru stands a few feet away, full of anger. Finally the girls make up their minds, take their things to the cashier. Nesbitt pays with one of his credit cards, doesn't even look at the bill, though the girls have bought unstintingly; I don't think they could have chosen anything more expensive.

Dru pushes us all toward the escalator, says, "Get moving! Come on!" We've been here for over an hour, and they're about to close; the PA speakers are already saying, "Ladies and gentlemen, please complete your purchases." We go down to pay for my things and Dru's. The two girls giggle between themselves, glance frivolously at the clerk, who is tapping out the bill and closing the cash register for the day. Nesbitt looks around as if he were naked, says, "What about me?"

We make a last attempt, running to the sports department, and Elaine finds a pair of yellow basketball shoes. Nesbitt doesn't seem convinced, says, "Didn't they say *clothes*?" Dru pulls him toward the last cash desk still open, says, "Shoes are fine. It's the idea that counts."

We cross again the empty parking garage, go back to the

hotel with our big plastic bags. The lobby now is half occupied by men and women with badges on their lapels, groups of photographers, vaguely alarmed bystanders. The hotel's other activities are virtually overwhelmed by this single-purposed presence; they continue in an increasingly marginal way. Elaine asks a policeman what's going on; the policeman says, "The vice president's coming in a couple of hours."

We head for the elevators, and the voice over the PA system is saying, "Mr. Resnik wanted on the telephone, please. Telephone call for Mr. Resnik." Dru gapes and answers; he listens with a worried look, nods a couple of times, hangs up, stands there. He comes to us, says, "Listen, we have to find a shirt or a jacket or some kind of suit that's yellow, for Jack."

"Why?" Jack says, filled with alarm. He turns and looks into the lobby, says, "Do they already know I haven't found anything?"

Dru scratches his temple, says, "He treated me like a kind of dumb schoolboy. He asked if we had clothes in our colors, and I said yes, and he said it's not true for yellow."

Elaine finds her devout tone again, says, "It's fundamental to follow the instructions literally; every detail has great significance."

"Well, why didn't you think of that before, since you're so smart?" Dru says to her.

A man with an earplug and a transmitter in his hand stares at us from near the elevators; he follows our gestures. We probably don't look too trustworthy, anxious and uncertain and frantic as we are. Rickie looks at her watch, says, "At this hour, on Saturday evening, all the shops are closed."

"There must be a way to find a yellow jacket somewhere," Nesbitt says in a panicked voice. I don't know what he thinks the business of the colored clothes means at this point, but he surely looks like somebody left without shelter a few minutes before the bomb.

We try the hotel boutiques, but there's nothing; we try the hotel department store, search among the aspirin and portable razors and postcards and souvenir towels. We ask the salesgirl; Dru says to her, "It's very important." She shakes her head, probably thinks we're a group of idiots excited over some kind of treasure hunt.

Nesbitt and Rickie, all the same, take a second turn around the shelves. Dru persists with the salesgirl; in a pathetic-ironic tone he says to her, "You've *got* to help us; we're desperate."

The salesgirl seems intrigued by this; she smiles. She's pretty, has an alert look.

Dru says to her, "This is serious; if our friend doesn't find a yellow coat, we're in trouble."

The girl says, "I'm sorry. I see it's serious."

Dru immediately exploits this opening, adopts now almost the tone of a suitor. He says, "Can't you help us then, pretty and sensitive as you are?" He can't resist this kind of first-contact flirtation, even at a moment like this; I believe he enjoys it more than any subsequent developments. He says, "Don't you know anybody who could lend us a yellow coat?"

The girl laughs, shakes her head. She's *very* pretty, actually, not tall but well shaped, with dark eyes, wavy brown hair. She says, "My boyfriend *does* have a yellow windbreaker. But he's in Mexico for a week."

"Couldn't you borrow it?" Dru says; he brushes her arm with his hand. He has an almost perfect way of becoming confidential in no time, only slightly insidious, without too much pressure.

The girl smiles, says, "Without telling him anything?"

"Yes," Dru says. He looks her in the eyes, says, "When he gets back, he won't even notice." Behind him, Elaine begins to be irritated; she pretends to be greatly interested in a display of brushes.

The salesgirl looks at Dru in the same way, says, "All right." Now that I can see her better, she is *incredibly* pretty; she moves with a concentrated, honed grace.

Dru says to her, "You're wonderful, you've saved us." He leans over and gives her a kiss on the cheek, and I have a twinge of absurd jealousy, I'd like to pull him back. He asks her, "What's your name?"

"Sashy," she says.

Dru introduces her to me and Elaine; to Nesbitt and Rickie, returning from their futile patrol. He says, "This is Sashy and she's found us a yellow jacket."

"Really?" Nesbitt says; he leans on the counter.

Rickie points a finger at Sashy's blouse, she says, "Gray."

Sashy's skirt is gray, too; all four of us stare at her. She doesn't seem sure of the reason for our interest. She says, "What's so funny about that?"

"It's a beautiful color," Dru says cautiously, as if he were speaking in code.

"Thanks," Sashy says. An Oriental gentleman peers in to ask her for digestive tablets; she signals to him that she'll be right there, says to us, "I get off in twenty minutes."

We go up and leave our packages in Dru's room; we come back down a little before eight. Sashy turns over the job to a pale, thin girl, slips on a jacket the same color as the rest of her clothes; she tells us to follow her. In the lobby the crowd waiting for the vice president has now taken over three-quarters of the space, and continues occupying more. Sashy picks her way through the people, past the hotel office of TWA, along the corridors leading to the elevators for the garage. She turns every now and then to give us a glance, she smiles. Dru and Nesbitt and I follow her, enchanted by her way of walking; by her profile when she stops at the doors of the elevator and waits. The elevator opens; two plainclothesmen record us with professional eyes before they come out.

Up in the garage, Sashy leads us among the cars to a Volkswagen minibus, opens the side door, reaches in and rummages in a couple of bags. Dru and Nesbitt and I watch her, not saying anything. I believe Elaine and Rickie realize how attracted we are to her; they remain in the background with faces of pretended boredom.

Sashy takes out a yellow windbreaker, hands it to Nesbitt, says, "Here you are."

Nesbitt says, "Thanks," spreads it out in his hands; it's an electric yellow, satin, with the words *Tact Cons* written in black on the back.

"My boyfriend plays baseball," Sashy says; she closes the door again.

We look at one another for a second in the garage, and it seems terrible that she should go away now. Dru says to her, "Sashy, you have to help us now with one other thing. We need to find some musical instruments right away."

"What instruments?" Sashy says, her back against the minibus. She has a hard and ironic tone now, a young gun moll dressed for some reason in respectable clothes. Rickie seems uselessly big and exuberant beside her; Elaine, cold, with washed-out features.

Dru says, "I don't know. I think I'd like one of those electronic keyboards that make all different sounds."

"An electric guitar for me," Rickie says. She mimes the playing of an electric guitar, but she's clumsy as a little girl overstuffed with vitamins, and nobody is really looking at her.

It irks me just to have her near me, it irritates and embarrasses me. I don't know why, but I've never been so fickle in these things.

Sashy says, "I know a place that's always open"; she motions us to get into the minibus. We all pile inside; she drives rapidly out of the garage, out of Beverly Hills. Dru, seated on her right, continues to look at her, he says again, "You're wonderful, Sashy."

"Cut it out," she says without turning to him; she zigzags among the cars.

Dru says, "But it's the truth." He looks saddened now; perhaps at the thought that, according to You, she's Nesbitt's girl. To me, it seems a crime; I only hope somebody misunderstood. I look at her from behind, try to absorb the little movements with which she turns the wheel and shifts gears, the elegant and light way she raises her foot from the clutch. Nesbitt is also quite careful; Rickie and Elaine look outside.

Sashy stops in a concrete lot off Pico Boulevard; she jumps out. There is a self-service gas station, with a car-wash tunnel and a glass cabin from which two attendants check the meters of the pumps. Sashy goes to talk with one of the men; we all follow her. She says to him, "I have to see Marvin. Curtis sent me."

The attendant looks at her through the glass, looks at us behind her. The glass is bulletproof; there is a rotating cup for the money. He says, "Just a minute"; presses the button, comes outside. He studies us all once more, motions us to follow him. We go behind the car-wash tunnel, into a little office with a desk and a water cooler, a couple of calendars with naked women and automobiles on the walls. The attendant talks over an intercom, says, "Marvin, there's some people for you. Friends of Curtis."

Sashy looks around, her hands in the pockets of her jacket.

She has a delightful manner; I'd run off with her immediately, without giving it a moment's thought.

The attendant waits. He says, "Okay," hangs up. He goes and touches something behind the water cooler; a wall slides for about three feet, revealing a passage. He signals us to go ahead.

At the end there's a door; Sashy knocks and a black guy opens, says, "Curtis has owed me *fifteen hundred dollars* for three months. I can't even get him on the phone; he has them say he's out. He made me give him a '54 Stratocaster worth five times what I charged him, and I haven't seen it since. He comes and says to me, all pathetic, that I've got to help him because he has a contract for the Mick Jagger record, he absolutely has to have the right guitar, and then he disappears in this lousy way."

Dru says, "We'll pay everything. Don't worry. We have to buy some instruments. We need them right away."

The black guy looks at him, even more hostile than before; he looks at Sashy. He says, "Who's this guy? He goes around paying other people's debts? What you call a philanthropist?"

Sashy goes over to him, says to him in a low voice, "We're all thirteen twenty-one six," or something of the sort.

The black guy's expression changes in the space of a second; he motions us to come in. He says, "You can call me Marvin. What do you need?" He leads us along a passage, opens a door into a big room full of electric and acoustic guitars propped on stands and cases one next to the other. We step inside to get a better look, and they all seem of high quality, even though they're jumbled together so casually. Once I worked on a TV series about a fifties band, and guitars like these cost us a fortune just to hire by the week. There are vintage Fenders and Gibsons that I think would drive any rock musician or collector out of his mind, old Martins with their wood darkened, Epiphones and Guilds and semiacoustic Gretches that look as if they'd been taken from some revival photographs.

Marvin leads us to another room full of electronic keyboards and sequencers and synthesizers, long black boxes full of buttons and cursors and meters and LEDs and little sophisticated legends and numbers. Dru roams around the piles of material, taps an occasional mute key.

And it's a bit like it was with the clothes in the department store, plus the fact that none of us, except Rickie, has the slightest idea how to play. We look at all these extraordinary instruments as mere objects, judge them on the basis of shape and color more than anything else. We make futile approaches, attempts at juxtapositions. Rickie chooses a white electric guitar in the form of a Z, slings it around her neck, goes to Dru and asks him how it looks on her. Dru says, "Fine" almost without looking at her. I take a semiacoustic with a round body of flamed maple, a neck of ebony inlaid with mother-of-pearl frets, the keys plated with gold. It's a guitar for a fifty-year-old country-and-western player, but so opulent that it's hard to resist. Dru asks for the keyboard nearest him, says, "So long as we don't stay here all night."

Elaine starts asking Marvin information about the sample keyboards; she says, "Which one is the *best*?" Marvin tries to explain to her that they have different qualities; she says, "I mean the *absolute* best." She ends up taking the most expensive, long as a piano, hard to carry. Nesbitt comes back from another room with a tenor sax; he seems fascinated by the shiny brass. It's absurd, these five incompetents grabbing instruments with which a group of professionals could earn enough to live on for years. I believe Sashy is thinking this, because she looks at us with folded arms; she smiles.

Dru says to her, "You haven't chosen yet?"

"How do I come into it?" she says.

"What do you mean?" Dru says. "You're Gray; you have to have an instrument so you can play it at midnight." He forces her to choose something; he insists until she picks out an electric bass.

Marvin produces the proper amplifiers and other indispensable accessories, cables and straps and picks and cases; he piles everything by the door. He sits at a table to add up the bill, tapping on a calculator; he checks two or three times. He seems puzzled by the total amount, passes the slip of paper to Nesbitt. Nesbitt takes out a credit card; Marvin pushes it back with open palms, turns hostile, says, "No, no." Nesbitt shows him an ID, telephone number, finally manages to pay with a check. Marvin says to leave everything there and bring the minibus into the car-wash tunnel. The attendant comes to start it, motions us to remain seated inside. We pass through the jets of water and the foam, the rotating brushes. Sashy laughs, drums a rhythm on the wheel. When the cycle is about to end, and the drying gusts of hot air begin, the attendant comes and bangs on the side door, rapidly loads all the instruments. Sashy drives out; we go back to the hotel in the sparkling minibus crammed with stuff.

In the driveway there is a line of three black limousines that glide along slowly and stop under the marquee; explosions of flashbulbs at either side of the glass doors. A tall man dressed in blue gets out of the middle car, rapidly walks through a corridor of plainclothesmen and photographers and supporters and curious bystanders who all applaud, crammed together. Elaine says, "Election chances, zero." It's not clear on what knowledge of the situation she bases this statement.

We unload the instruments and amplifiers in the confusion, drag them through the crowd like a rock group with serious organization problems.

Upstairs we deposit everything in Dru's room, look at one another. Dru says, "Maybe you could all go to Dave's room; I'd like to be alone for a while." He looks strained and tired, his face pale, as he accompanies us to the door and shuts it again.

In my room we distribute ourselves among straight chairs and easy chairs and the bed and the bathroom. Rickie turns on the TV: the vice president's arrival at the hotel five minutes ago, filmed from the point of view opposite the one we had. Sashy says, "Look," points to our minibus behind the big black cars.

I try to breathe calmly

I try to breathe calmly, not to let the situation get too much of a hold on me. I say, "We've done everything you wanted."

The voice goes on, as if not taking this in; it says, "The succession of events has been positive in this phase, Green; the difficulties encountered are not cause for concern, therefore we approve."

I decipher the words one by one as they pass through the receiver, the meaning of the whole sentence gradually as the words complete it, and I'm angered by this deaf and peremptory tone. I'm angered for having made myself so available. I say, "See here, why do you always speak in the plural? How many of you are there?"

"From our point of view it is unimportant to make distinctions in terms of quantity, Green," the voice says, each word distinct, as if by itself it had an incredible importance. And it isn't at all an electronic voice, the voice of a Japanese science-fiction animated film; the words are charged and expanded to the limit of their possibilities, then made to take on a uniform cadence; every time I say something, the voice is already answering, but its answer doesn't deviate from the direction it was already taking. It's as if it doesn't want to lower itself to my level, or else it foresees what I am going to say and is following a predetermined path, or else it is actually able to make me say what it wants, creating both my part and its own, like an impatient scriptwriter.

I say, "I'm glad you've become interested in me, and it all seems very fascinating, but I don't exactly understand the purpose of this contact."

The voice again overlaps mine without allowing me to finish; it says, "Your perspective, Green, must be reversed in order for you to perceive the form and the reasons of this communication." It is, in purely acoustical terms, implacable, persistent, and without nuances, as if it had never been grazed by even the most remote doubt.

"The fact is, however, that I don't understand your language and almost nothing of what has happened," I say. I'm fed up with this bogus dialogue, with waiting for the voice to decide on the moment for explanations.

The voice says, "The greatest difficulty in the present communication, Green, consists in making the content of the messages comprehensible to those who receive them." And I sense concern beneath the imperturbable tone, beneath the dull, bureaucratic choice of words.

"But what are the messages?" I say, and I realize I'm succumbing to agitation, no matter how hard I try to remain detached. I say, "What is the message?"

The voice is silent. There is faint crackling on the line,

201

static, distant voices in other languages, as if an intercontinental connection had been left open.

I can't force myself to wait; a panic rises in me at the thought that the communication has been cut off; I say, "What is the message? That we are all making the wrong use of the world and of ourselves by destroying and consuming almost everything we could and building horrible containers for lives and activities, and debasing and reducing to slavery the other animals and the plants, and imprisoning our sensations in machines and deals and trade, until they've become too different from what they could have been?" It's ridiculous; the words come from me before I have time to think them; they form on their own, like uncontrolled impressions.

The voice says, "We approve, Green, and we are assisting you."

"But will you clarify something for us at midnight?" I say. "Will you give us a more precise idea?" I am less overwhelmed than a few seconds ago, but it seems to me that I am still speaking at an incredible speed, almost without sounds.

"Your desire to foresee the course of events is irrelevant from our point of view, because the future and the past are at the same distance," the voice says.

"You mean you already know everything that will happen?" I say. "You see our future from above, like a railroad track?"

"Time isn't linear," the voice says. Again it seems to be making an effort to be clearer, even if it still doesn't seem to listen to my words. It says, "There are two contiguous futures; you may pass from one to the other only if you perceive them."

"Then the future isn't inevitable?" I say.

"Everything that you people haven't constructed is much less inevitable than you think, Green," the voice says.

And immediately afterward, for a moment, it seems to me

that I am before a vista, and I can go further by exerting a minimum of extra effort, but the mere idea of effort is enough to weigh me down, drag me lower, shut off the prospect.

The voice says, "The message, Green, is the story you will tell." I may be mistaken, but it seems to me that there is a touch of cordiality beneath his tone, distant but perceptible.

I have come back to earth, my panic of the void has completely passed. I say, "Then you want me to make a film about what has happened?" I also utter each word distinctly, as if I were talking with some childish character in a TV film, a kitsch puppet activated by remote control.

"The succession of the events and of their content will be depicted in your work," the voice says, as if it needs to translate for its files what it has said to me unofficially.

"I'm not sure how that would come out," I say. "There are so many things that aren't clear, and some elements are out of proportion; there are whole characters that I don't know what to do with. The film would be a mess. Nobody would be convinced." I don't even know if I am trying to evade responsibility or if I'm speaking in purely professional terms or if I'm too tired and confused to continue this unbalanced dialogue. But I go on, since I'm involved in it now. I say, "And what's more, I don't believe I'll ever have any real certainties, whatever may happen to me. I mean, even at this moment I should be convinced, but I'm not; maybe I will be at midnight, but not now. I'm not the ideal person for your message. I'm sorry, but you've made the wrong choice. It seems to me that almost everything is possible, but I don't believe I'll ever be completely sure of any one possibility."

"This, Green, is why we sought each other out," the voice says. And I could swear that at this moment it has an amused

tone; there is a subtle electromagnetic vibration of amusement that arrives directly inside my head.

I say, "Listen to me for a moment," but there is no longer anyone at the other end: the line is open, full of little, irrelevant sounds.

The blue jacket is a pretty good fit

The blue jacket is a pretty good fit; I've never had one so sober and so well made in my life. While I was about it, maybe I should have got myself also a real pair of shoes to wear instead of these trainers. Nesbitt, on the other hand, is more informal than he's ever been, with his yellow basketball shoes and the satin windbreaker with *Tact Cons* written on it. He takes a few embarrassed steps around the room, says to Sashy, "Am I too ridiculous?"

"No, no," she says, leaning against the window. "You're different, mostly."

"Different," Nesbitt says; he tries at least to fix his hair.

Elaine and Rickie finish putting on their makeup, swish in their new dresses between the bathroom mirror and the one in the closet opposite the bed; they trade eye shadow and lipstick and mascara. Rickie's dress isn't even properly pink; it's in various shades that go from salmon to magenta; Elaine's makes her look like a human gardenia, quite glamorous. Sashy has simply taken a shower and put on the clothes she was wearing before, and she's ten times as attractive as the other two put together. Nesbitt and I try to be near her, on the slightest pretext we talk to her about anything at all. I can't understand how I was so captivated by Elaine, and by Rickie, now that I see Sashy.

At ten past eleven, when all of us are ready, we go and knock on Dru's door. He opens it in his shirtsleeves and without his shoes, looking even more shaken than he did when we left him. He shuts himself in the bathroom while we wander around among the amplifiers and instruments, says, "I'll be right there."

He comes out again after a couple of minutes, pretty much pulled together; he slips on the green jacket, buttons it. He says, "What do you think we should do?" He is rapidly turning nervous again, looks around; from the closet he takes Camado's stick, props it against a wall.

Sashy points to the amplifiers, says, "Maybe we could start hooking them up, for a start."

We look around, unplug the table lamp and the standing lamp, but there aren't enough outlets. The three girls look in every corner, along the floorboards. Rickie says, "We need a double socket."

Dru says to me, "Run down and buy a couple." He changes his mind as I'm heading for the door; he says, "Wait, I'll come with you."

Down in the lobby, all the vice president's people are shut up in the convention hall; only some security men have been left outside, and a couple of uniformed policemen and a little group of photographers. Amplified voices filter through the door; sounds of collective laughter and applause. Beyond the outer glass wall, a line of limousines is waiting.

We go toward the hotel supermarket, and a man with a thin face blocks our path, says, "Dru Resnik?"

"Yes?" Dru says.

The thin-faced man says, "I'm a great fan of yours, I don't even know myself how many times I've seen your pictures." He smiles, holds out his hand. Just behind him are his ugly wife and an ugly fifteen-year-old daughter, all teeth.

"I'm delighted," Dru says. He points to me, says, "My assistant."

The guy shakes my hand, too. He must be slightly drunk, as well as full of admiration for Dru. He says, "I'm a Swissair pilot; I fly the transoceanic route."

"Then I hope to fly with you sometime," Dru says, and makes a gesture of disengagement. We almost run off, before the eyes of the intrusive little family.

We buy three double sockets from the girl who has taken Sashy's place. Dru looks to see if she also has some role in this story, but she seems totally insignificant.

We go back into the lobby, and the Swissair pilot by the door of the convention hall touches a photographer's arm, points at Dru. And a moment later *all* the photographers, who have been dozing while they wait, suddenly wake up and run after us. They cry, "Mr. Resnik! Wait a minute! Just a minute, Mr. Resnik!" They explode flashbulbs like lunatics, circle around Dru, close in on him. They shove, try to get ahead of one another, gain space by elbowing; they produce frantic little clicks in the half-empty lobby. Dru puts his back against a wall, lets himself be photographed like a criminal trapped by the police. Then he recovers, assumes a couple of photograph poses, a couple of professional smiles; he changes profile under the rapid lights. He tries to disengage himself and get away; the photographers block his path, yell, "Just one more!"

I'm thinking how to pull him out, but the doors of the convention hall open, and some people begin to emerge; all the photographers turn around, run over there.

We slip into the elevator. Dru says, "Son-of-a-bitch pilot, bastard."

Up in his room, we connect the last of the amplifiers to the outlets, the instruments to the amplifiers; we look at the instruments closely, as if that were enough to get an idea of what you have to do to play them. Dru and Elaine need legs or supports for their keyboards; they finally set them, one against the other, on opposite sides of the bed. Nesbitt checks his saxophone, tries to figure out where to place his fingers. Rickie gives him advice, but when she tries to hold the saxophone, it's obvious she's bluffing. Elaine can't regulate the volume of her amplifier, which keeps sizzling; she turns dials at random. There is this tangle of little wires, all these cumbersome and heavy and expensive instruments, and we don't even know what to do with them. We stand up and sit down and stand up again to find the right position, we adjust straps and meters without the slightest notion of what we're doing, and yet the air is becoming saturated with expectation. I try tuning my guitar with Sashy's bass, but Rickie distracts me every two seconds.

Nesbitt says, "Three minutes to midnight."

Dru accidentally touches his keyboard: a spiral of spatial, reechoed sounds. He says, "Wouldn't it be better if we at least turned off this lousy light?"

I set down the guitar, which emits a hollow wave through the amplifier, I go to turn off the light. At first you can hardly see a thing, except for the little red lights of the amplifiers, the little green lights of the two keyboards on the bed. Then from the window comes a tender opalescent glow that spreads through three-quarters of the room, enough to cast shadows from us and the instruments.

We remain still in this subluminous haze, among faint sounds: the hum of electric wires, buzz of amplifiers, rustling of clothes, scrape of soles and heels on the carpet, breathing, muffled voices from other rooms, distant croaking of TV sets, barely audible passage of elevators. We wait, completely concentrated on waiting, and nothing happens.

After perhaps ten minutes, Dru says, "Let's try playing."

But we aren't even vaguely *close* to playing; we are only six separate sources of discordant sounds, which clash and intersect and drown one another without any pattern. Rickie and I make some wretched attempts at metallic chords on the guitars, off pitch and out of tempo; Nesbitt almost bursts his lungs with his saxophone, producing hoarse coughs without any shape; Dru and Elaine press keys at random; they activate uncontrollable electronic imitations of violins and accordions and brass and xylophones with vibrato. Sashy, at least, manages to play a timid scale of bass blues, but she proceeds on her own as if she were deaf, doesn't even try to go along with the overall lack of form. It's a kind of farce, not amusing; far worse than we could have imagined.

Dru shouts, "Stop! Stop!" It takes us a few seconds of noise to stop. Dru says, "This is impossible. We're disgusting." He seems surprised by this ruin, aghast.

Rickie says, "I have to tune up, I'm sorry."

"It's not a question of tuning," Dru says. "This stuff is

awful. It's *horrifying*. Let's try to concentrate, dammit. Let's make an *effort*." He tries to recondition us in the right atmosphere, as he does with actors on the set when they are totally off-key; he lets about thirty seconds go by, says, "Let's try again, *softly*."

We try again, more cautiously, at a lower volume and with sparse sounds, but in a very little while it's almost worse than before. We seem like a group of idiots, or people deliberately acting like idiots: each doggedly at his instrument and full of misguided commitment, with his little repertory of musical errors and tricks and self-quotations. We drag out the first notes we happen to find, make them clash with one another, stir up waves of resonant desolation. We persist, let ourselves be carried adrift, as if it were only a matter of holding out until a waterspout of inspiration comes and lifts us up or bears us away, far from this disaster.

There is a knock at the door.

We all stop playing at the same moment: there is a sudden thickening of atmosphere that arrests the sounds like a mute.

The knocking is repeated, louder. Dru says, "It's not locked," in a slightly unsteady tone. We are all motionless in the semidarkness; our shadows breathe close to the instruments.

The door opens; a large form appears against the luminous background of the corridor. Elaine makes a start; Nesbitt says, "What the hell . . . " I turn to look at the window, with a couple of mental flashes of me jumping out onto the balcony below.

The heavy figure takes two steps into the room, says, "Isn't there any light here?" The voice is liquid, gurgling.

Dru says, "Sashy, turn it on." Sashy gets up, stumbles over a wire, sprawls on the floor. We are stiff, paralyzed.

Sashy gets up again, finds the switch. She turns it on, and

there is a heavyset policeman or security guard in a blue uniform by the door, with a hat and a gilt badge and a gun belt and a revolver in a holster. He looks at us, puzzled, looks at the floor cluttered with amplifiers and empty cases and instruments, the tangle of wires. He signals vaguely toward the corridor, says: "Some of the other rooms complained. It's twelve-thirty . . . "

Dru rises slowly from his keyboard; it takes him, I believe, a few seconds to put the real situation in the place of the one he had anticipated. He says, "Of course. We've finished anyway." He switches off the keyboard, the amplifier.

The policeman says, "Good night" in a low voice, withdraws into the corridor, shuts the door again.

Dru takes Camado's stick, shuts it in the closet again; he goes and draws aside the curtain, peers out. He has an incredibly disappointed look, almost without expression. He turns to observe us as if we were really poor idiots, seated here and there in the room at instruments we don't know how to play.

We turn off everything, pull out the plugs, put the instruments in their cases, coil up the wires. There is this atmosphere of a failed space launch; we avoid looking at one another's faces. When we've finished packing up everything and there are no longer any excuses for staying here, Dru says, "Let's get out of this lousy hotel, at least."

Then we are in the car and going to I don't know which restaurant that stays open very late, and Nesbitt at the wheel is seized by a kind of convulsive gasping. He makes an effort to breathe normally, but he can't; he slows down. We are seated in the big, padded Mercedes, with assumed faces expressing suitable nuances; we turn and look at him as he stops the car and puts one hand to his mouth, succumbs; he is laughing.

"What the hell seems so funny to you?" Dru says to him,

full of rage. But a second later he has an involuntary smile, and it takes over before he can stifle it. He laughs in a semirepressed way, then out loud, almost hysterically. Sashy also laughs, Elaine, Rickie, me. We laugh like mad, all six of us; the car fills with gasps and coughing and guttural sounds and catchings of breath and squeaks and fragmentary attempts to say something. Nesbitt is bent over the wheel, Dru against Elaine with her legs drawn up, Sashy and Rickie swaying to themselves and to me. It is a current of high tension that passes through us, it's painful to the stomach and the lungs, it presses against the heart, brings tears to the eyes. We go on as if we will never be able to stop; I haven't the slightest idea how long it can last.

When it seems the laughter has lost intensity, Nesbitt drives off again slowly, still sniffing and coughing; but ten yards farther on we are again completely swept away; he has to pull to the side once more so as not to lose control of the wheel. We sit there laughing and laughing like kids, with cars passing us and creating air pockets.

It takes at least ten minutes before the thing diminishes, and when Nesbitt again pulls out into the nighttime traffic, we are still so dazed that a pickup truck nearly runs into us. The driver brakes, honks, makes furious gestures, but none of us can take him seriously. We laugh at this, too; Nesbitt drives, zigzagging.

We arrive at the ocean, head north. Dru looks out, says, "It's incredible."

"What?" Sashy says, in a voice hoarse from laughing.

"The *effort* we put into it," Dru says. There is still a hint of disappointment beneath his tone; barely a trace, but it's there. For the rest, I believe we all feel light, glad to be together in this car in this city at this hour.

Nesbitt drives along the shore, looking for the restaurant; he can't remember where it is. Sashy and Rickie and Elaine give him conflicting advice; they point in various directions. It's not the ideal moment for finding a place; none of us can concentrate. Nesbitt turns on the radio, and there is a lively song, with a nice, fast bass line. Dru turns up the volume; Rickie beats time with her hands.

Farther ahead, Dru points to a ramshackle bar on our right; he says, "Let's stop here. Let's skip the restaurant."

Inside, we order six cheeseburgers and six beers. The only other customers are two girls, motorcyclists, seated at one table, and a fat man standing and eating while he watches a TV on a shelf. The counterman prepares the cheeseburgers with automatic movements, a stylized routine in the white light of the neon. We observe him while we lean on the counter, exhausted and pensive, as if we had already achieved a great deal for today. Through the panes behind us, the headlights of the cars can be seen passing along the ocean.